Hᴀᴠᴇ ʏᴏᴜ ᴇᴠᴇʀ ᴡɪsʜᴇᴅ ʏᴏᴜ ᴄᴏᴜʟᴅ ʙᴇ ᴀ ᴋɪᴅ again? H...
hood whi...
up and fa...
mentary c...
demarcati...

Yet nowadays we hear a lot about the need for learning to express our "inner child," that creative, open, spontaneous, oft-buried part of ourselves. Being a closet free spirit, I like that notion. I admire adventurous souls who celebrate life and thumb their noses at dour, conventional drudgery.

Pip LeBaron, the heroine of *Fly with Me*, was a child prodigy who never had the opportunity to be "just a kid." When she goes on a quest to recapture her lost childhood, who better to be her Pygmalion than an older version of Peter Pan? Sawyer Hayes, a free-spirited, impish charmer, is made for the role.

The Peter Pan syndrome is a modern pop-psych term for immature men who have never grown up. But is "growing up" all it's cracked up to be? And exactly what is "growing up"? Why do we have to trade the Peter Pan joie de vivre for the serious weight of responsibility? What price *maturity*?

Adulthood can be fun. It's all in the attitude.

I've cast Pip and Sawyer, two social misfits, in a story of romance, laughter, and discovery with variants of the villainous Hook, lost boys, and Nana thrown in. Since I've always adored myths, fairy-tales, and fantasy, I loved writing it. Enjoy!

Jan Hudson

WHAT ARE *LOVESWEPT* ROMANCES?

They are stories of true romance and touching emotion. We believe those two very important ingredients are constants in our highly sensual and very believable stories in the LOVESWEPT line. Our goal is to give you, the reader, stories of consistently high quality that may sometimes make you laugh, sometimes make you cry, but are always fresh and creative and contain many delightful surprises within their pages.

Most romance fans read an enormous number of books. Those they truly love, they keep. Others may be traded with friends and soon forgotten. We hope that each LOVESWEPT romance will be a treasure—a "keeper." We will always try to publish

LOVE STORIES YOU'LL NEVER FORGET
BY AUTHORS YOU'LL ALWAYS REMEMBER

The Editors

Loveswept 663

FLY WITH ME

JAN HUDSON

BANTAM BOOKS
NEW YORK · TORONTO · LONDON · SYDNEY · AUCKLAND

FLY WITH ME

A Bantam Book / January 1994

If you would be interested in receiving protective vinyl covers for your
Loveswept books, please write to this address for information:

Loveswept
Bantam Books
P.O. Box 985
Hicksville, NY 11802

ISBN 0-553-44433-6

Published simultaneously in the United States and Canada

For Ginna Gray

ONE

Pip dipped her brush into the can and carefully stroked the marine white enamel onto the side of the aging houseboat. Painting, along with most activities these days, was a new experience for Marguerite Elizabeth "Pip" LeBaron, Ph.D., but she'd read two instruction books that covered the subject in detail.

The day was hot for April. Sweat beaded above the full curve of her upper lip. It trickled from under her floppy hat, plastering tendrils of black hair to her forehead and making her red, heart-shaped sunglasses slide down into the blob of zinc oxide protecting her peeling nose.

She climbed down to move the stepladder

and gave her flushed face a swipe with the tail of her oversized Houston Oilers jersey. After a quick swallow of Gatorade from the cooler on the deck, she flipped her long, thick braid over her shoulder, wiped her damp hands on the seat of her cutoffs, and climbed back up the ladder to get on with her painting.

This was one of the projects she had listed in her *Outline for Accelerated Remediation of Social =Development*, and she was determined to finish before the Strahan twins across the lake got home from school. Friday was the afternoon they reserved for baseball practice, and she needed to work on her swing.

Pip painted the same way she did everything else—with intense, single-minded concentration. So immersed was she in making precise strokes with her brush, she failed to notice the fish jumping in the lake, making widening circles on the sun-shimmered surface, or the silvery schools of minnows darting in the algae-laden shallows under the pier. She missed the calls of the waterfowl and the whisper of the breeze playing through the tall pines and the spring-fragrant leaves of oak and sweetgum on the point.

Totally engrossed in the rhythmic dip, slap, slap, slap of enamel on wood, only a tiny part of her awareness registered the loud whir of a helicopter overhead or noted its landing on the pad at the big lake house beyond the trees. She wouldn't have heard the footsteps on the wooden pier a few minutes later if she hadn't stopped to move the ladder and take another swig from the jug in the cooler.

It was probably Nan checking on her, she thought as she spied her uneaten lunch resting in its Ziploc bag atop the ice. Pip shrugged and picked up the paintbrush again. She'd eat later. Nan, more like a doting grandmother than a housekeeper, would be furious with her. Pip could almost hear her scolding, "One of these days you're gonna dry up and blow away. You ain't big enough now to make a decent meal for a mosquito."

But when Pip, an excuse already forming in her agile mind, glanced toward the gangplank, instead of Nan she saw two men: a young one in casual clothes and a middle-aged one in a business suit.

"Ahoy, there," the young one said.

At first he seemed quite ordinary. He was dressed in faded jeans, a rumpled green windbreaker, and scruffy Reeboks. A well-worn green baseball cap was crammed over a thatch of reddish-brown hair. But it wasn't his attire that captured her attention. Something startling in his eyes—bold, brilliant green, and laughter-creased—caught and held hers.

At that moment an incredible thing happened to Pip. An absolutely incredible thing.

For the first time in all her twenty-six years, Pip LeBaron *saw* a man. Even with her extensive vocabulary she couldn't have explained exactly what it was about him that was different, but he seemed to exude a magical aura of appeal of such magnitude that she could only stand rooted to the deck with her mouth hanging open. He said something and flashed a smile as bright as the noon sun on Lake Conroe, but for the life of her she couldn't make his words register in the befuddled mess that had been her brain only moments ago.

She was as rigid as a petrified inhabitant of old Pompeii. Her paintbrush was poised in mid-air, and enamel dribbled down her arm to her elbow, then plopped onto the big toe poking out of a worn spot in her sneakers.

With a superhuman effort she managed to squeak out, "What?"

He laughed, flashing deep dimples. If he kept looking at her with those merry eyes, she felt as if she might dissolve into a puddle. He started to say something else, when the man with him stepped forward. The one in the green cap was enchanting, but this one seemed almost menacing. His hair and eyebrows were black and thick, as was the full mustache partly obscuring a downturned mouth. His face seemed carved into a permanent scowl. When he stepped closer, he towered at least a foot over her own nearly five feet. Pip slowly raised her head and peered up at him while Marine White Number 2 continued to dribble on her toe.

"We're looking for Dr. LeBaron," the gruff one said. "And we don't have time to dawdle. The housekeeper said she was here."

As some semblance of rational thought returned, she glanced at the younger man, who lazed against the rail, grinning from ear to ear, and another strange thing happened. For the first time in her life she became painfully aware of her appearance. Vanity reared its narcissistic head, and Pip was humiliated beyond belief that *he* should see her like this. She wanted to disappear through the cracks of the deck.

"She's not here," Pip blurted out. "She's gone to . . . to Denmark."

"Denmark?" The young one lifted his

brows and laughed with an engaging lilt
that curled Pip's paint-spattered toe and did
peculiar things to her pulse rate.

The older man snorted. "Denmark? Hog-
wash." He pulled a gold money clip from his
pocket and peeled off a bill. "Here's a dollar.
Be a good girl and find Dr. LeBaron for us.
Tell her we need to speak with her about
something very important. We'll be waiting
at the house."

He turned away, and Pip looked at the
dollar bill she held in her limp fingers. Her
humiliation grew tenfold. They'd thought she
was a kid.

Of course her diminutive size and cherubic
face had been a nuisance all her life, especially
since she always had been years younger than
her classmates and co-workers.

Pip made a disgusted snort. Why should
she care in any case? She was acting like
an awestruck adolescent, and according to
her carefully researched plan, that stage of
her development was months away yet. Still,
visions of a man who could turn her brain
mushy teased her rational arguments. She
sighed and stuck the dollar bill in her pocket.

A chuckle came from near the gangplank.
Pip's head shot up, and she was irritated

to discover the younger man lingering there, apparently enjoying her discomfort.

Pride overcame her earlier fascination with him. Lack of food had made her light-headed, she reasoned. Drawing herself up to her full four feet eleven and three-eighths inches, Pip gave the intruder the haughtiest glare possible. Perhaps the effect was lost behind the plastic valentine sunglasses, because he continued to grin at her. Pure devilment animated his eyes.

He reminded her a bit of a mischievous leprechaun—only bigger. Not that he was all that big, certainly not as imposing as his gruff cohort, but when he walked toward her, she noted that he was at least seven or eight inches taller than she.

"Exactly who are you? Where did you come from?" she asked.

"From the great whirlybird in the sky." When she only blinked and looked blank, he added, "The chopper. The helicopter. I'm the pilot." He sauntered closer, whipped off his cap, and executed a courtly bow. "Sawyer Hayes at your service, ma'am." The grin never left his face, but now his eyebrows twitched. "And you?"

"I'm Pip Le . . . I'm Pip."

"Ah. Dr. LeBaron, I presume?"

"Yes. Now if you'll excuse me, I have to finish this remaining wall. I'm on a tight schedule."

Before she could turn away, Sawyer grabbed her. "We'd better clean off your foot before you track paint all over the place."

Pip glanced down at the mess on her toe and grimaced at the telltale signs of her earlier idiocy.

"Here, let me take care of it." He doused a rag with thinner, knelt at her feet, and scrubbed away the drips. "There," he said giving a final swipe to the streaks on her arm. "That ought to do it. Got another brush?"

"Why?"

"Thought I'd help. Jobs like this are quicker with two—not to mention more fun."

She shrugged, located another brush and bucket, and the two of them started at opposite ends of the cabin wall. After a few minutes Pip stole a glance at Sawyer, who was whistling "Row, Row, Row Your Boat" and slapping enamel on the wood with amazing speed.

He caught her watching, and winked one bright-green eye. "You'd better get a move on, slowpoke, or I'm going to win."

"I didn't realize this was a competition."

"Yep," he said, painting even faster and not missing a stroke. Pip clenched her teeth and quickened her pace.

"I won!" Sawyer whooped, and dunked his brush into the can of thinner a split second before Pip finished.

"That's not fair! You had a head start."

"But I had a handicap. I did twice as much as you." He flipped open the cooler, pulled out the Gatorade, and handed the opened jug to Pip. After she'd had a swallow, he turned the drink up to take a big gulp.

He poked through the contents of the ice chest until he found a sandwich and gave Pip half. They sat on deck chairs, munched on ham and cheese, and surveyed their work.

"Why is that man here?"

"You mean Leonard Hooker? He's with Mirth, Incorporated." Sawyer got another sandwich and started toward Pip with it. When she shook her head, he stopped and said, "He wants to persuade you to take a job. I think you might find it interesting."

"I'm on a leave of absence for several months."

He wolfed down the food before he spoke again. "Why?"

"It's a long story."

"I've got all afternoon," Sawyer said, sliding down in his chair with his feet stuck out and his hands crossed over his stomach.

"I'm devoting my entire attention to my personal program for *Accelerated Remediation of Social Development*."

"What kind of program?"

"Accelerated Remediation of Social Development." Pip heaved a sigh and went on to explain. "You see, I've recently discovered that I'm socially retarded."

"You're *what*?"

"Socially retarded," Pip said in the same patient tone she used to tutor the eleven-year-old Strahan twins in math. When Sawyer cocked his eyebrows in a you've-got-to-be-putting-me-on expression, Pip pursed her full lips. "I assure you that it's true."

"And just how did you come to this amazing revelation?"

"Last fall I was one of the subjects in a dissertation study of child prodigies. The hypothesis was that by the time they are adults, their social development is severely impaired. My case is a classic example. My childhood was abnormal. Because I was academically gifted, my schoolmates were always much older than I, and I didn't fit in with their social activities. On the other hand, neither could I mix successfully with children of my own age, who were learning addition and the alphabet when I was mastering algebra and reading Shakespeare. I was a misfit."

Sawyer's animated expression became serious. "I'm sorry," he said quietly. "I've always been a little different myself. Were you unhappy as a child?"

"Not really. I wasn't even aware of what I'd missed until I read the study. Now it sounds rather tragic."

"You must have had wise and loving parents."

"I can't remember my parents. They died when I was two, in an accident in Chile. They were mining engineers. After that I went to live with my uncles. But, yes, they were very wise and loving substitute parents." Pip smiled as she thought of the bachelor professors who were suddenly the guardians of a toddler. "They were my only family except for my brother, who was already a freshman in college. Uncle Waldo and Uncle Emory did the best they could. They knew very little about children, but they hired Nan to look after me and taught me the things they knew. I grew up in an adult world of academics. We've always lived in a house only two blocks from Rice University, where they both still teach; Uncle Waldo is in the physics department, and Uncle Emory, mathematics. I left public school and started there when I was twelve."

They both sat quietly for a while and listened to the gentle lap of the water against the houseboat. Pip didn't usually talk about her personal life. Not that she was secretive; it was only that her mind and conversations had always, in the past, been concerned with the fascinating intricacies of mathematics or physics or mechanical engineering. Or her greatest love—computers.

There was nothing Pip couldn't do with a computer, from designing complex programs for NASA or the medical center to creating simple learning games for children. For the past several years there had been a long waiting list for her services as the top computer expert with her brother's consulting firm. The complicated projects that she immersed herself in, as well as the seminars she routinely taught at Rice, had occupied all of her time and attention. She had been content with her life.

Until she read psychologist Carol Venhuizen's dissertation and discovered she was socially retarded.

"You missed out on a lot," Sawyer said.

"So I've learned."

"What does that have to do with your not taking any jobs?"

"It's very simple. After I found that my personality was impaired, I did a great deal of research in psychosocial development. While there are critical periods—sort of the optimum times for learning and experiencing specific things—in the developmental process, it seems logical that one could simulate the pattern in some systematic way and hence bring the impaired areas up to normal."

Sawyer peered at her from under the bill of his cap. "I haven't the foggiest notion what you're talking about. What does all that mumbo jumbo have to do with taking a leave of absence?"

"I've devised a plan that will take all my time for a lengthy period. Since I missed so much in my social development, I'm starting over."

"How can you start over? Will that work?"

"Theoretically there's no reason why it shouldn't. As I said, I've done a great deal of research and, with Carol Venhuizen's assistance, designed what seems to be a workable strategy to simulate the social development. It's been only three months, and already I've progressed to late childhood. By interacting with the appropriate age groups I've mastered all the stages of play up to cooperative supplementary play, and I'm now engaged in experiencing Erik Erikson's fourth stage of psychosocial development; 'industry versus inferiority,'" Pip said, lifting her small chin with pride.

Sawyer's eyes crinkled in amusement, and his lips twitched as he fought to keep from laughing. For all her seriousness and ten-dollar words, Pip LeBaron was adorable. He had an almost irresistible urge to grab her by the hand, throw her in the chopper, and abscond with her to a faraway place.

"You've come that far, huh?" he said. "Sounds like you've really been having fun."

There was a long pause. The smug look on Pip's gamin face slowly dissolved into a sober, pensive one. Then her chin lifted again. "Why, of course I have. I'm involved in Girl Scouts, and I'm learning to play baseball, and tomorrow," she said with a curt nod for emphasis, "Nan is going to teach Sissy Strahan and me to make fudge."

Sawyer ducked his head to hide the grin that burst from its restraints. He had a notion that she wouldn't appreciate his amusement. And he didn't want to do anything to rankle her at this stage of the game because he had a strong hunch that he had met his match.

"So you can see, my time is totally devoted to my remediation program. You'll have to explain to your employer that it is impossible for me to take on any jobs for several months."

"Leonard's not my—"

Sawyer was interrupted by shouting from the lake. A small motorboat was heading toward them. Its occupants, a towheaded boy and girl in orange life jackets, waved and yelled at Pip. She returned their greeting and walked to the pier to await them.

"Thank you for your assistance with the painting," Pip said to Sawyer, who stood beside her. "You'll have to excuse me now. It's time for my baseball lesson."

Sawyer repositioned his cap, stuck his hands in the back pockets of his jeans, and rocked back on his heels. "I think I'll hang around for the game. I'm a pretty good catcher."

❖━━━━━━━━❖

"What do you mean I'm out?" Pip yelled up at Sawyer. "I didn't even swing at it!"

Sawyer bent down until his nose was almost touching hers and glared into the heart-shaped sunglasses. "You don't have to swing at it! Are you blind? It was right down the middle for a strike."

Pip slammed the bat to the ground and planted her fists on her hips. "It was not!"

"Was too!"

"Was not!"

Sawyer motioned with his thumb and shouted, "You're out. If you don't believe me, ask Mark or Sissy. Ask Leonard."

She had forgotten about him for a moment. A terrible sinking feeling came over her as she remembered the pitcher. Sawyer had badgered Leonard Hooker into doffing his coat, vest, and tie and joining the Strahan twins and them in the game. A furtive glance toward the sour-faced man standing on the makeshift mound made her want to slink away in shame over her behavior. He watched her as if she were a bug on a plate.

"I'm guess I'm not very good at this," Pip said quietly, swallowing the lump in her throat and looking down at the toes of her sneakers.

Sawyer threw his arm around her hunched shoulders. "Aw, you're doing fine. You just need a little more practice." He glanced at his watch. "It's about time for us to quit if the twins are going to make it home for supper. And Leonard and I need to get back to Houston."

Everyone said good-bye, and Pip gathered up the baseball equipment and stacked it on the porch. She was quiet all through dinner. Later she chose to walk down to the lake instead of watching the sitcoms on TV that all the kids loved. She couldn't even work up any enthusiasm for the Judy Blume book that was on her list of recommended reading.

The path was lit by tall vapor lights, which cast a golden glow over the trees and softly illuminated the houseboat docked at the landing. Pip strolled to the end of the pier and sat down, legs dangling over the edge and head resting against a mooring post. A faint breeze rippled the surface of the dark water and brought scents of fresh paint mingled with the distinctive smells of the lake. The evening was alive with the steady chirr and trill of tree frogs and crickets. Now and then there was a plop in the shimmering shadows as a fish jumped.

It had been a strange day. Until that afternoon Pip had been perfectly content with her project. Learning that there were children of about the right age among the permanent residents across the lake, she had borrowed a client's vacation house for the current phase of her scheme. And for the past few weeks things had gone well. Mark and Sissy Strahan, or rather their parents, had been delighted to trade Pip's tutoring the youngsters in math for an opportunity to share social activities with the twins and their friends. Everything was going according to plan, and she was confident that her theory was working.

Until that afternoon. Something about Sawyer Hayes and Leonard Hooker's visit had sown seeds of disquiet, muddled her thinking, interrupted her momentum. Instead of focusing on her program, her mind kept wandering to thoughts of Sawyer.

With no provocation, pictures of Sawyer's quick smile and his laughing eyes kept flashing through her head. Even remembering the odd way he looked at her made her skin feel peculiar—as if she'd rubbed it vigorously with a loofah sponge.

Mostly she recalled his laughter. How it captivated. How it came so quickly and so often, as if he were party to some private joke or source of secret merriment.

When she considered it, she wondered if he'd been laughing at her. Had he been ridiculing her? A knot formed in her stomach at the notion.

For the first time Pip doubted the wisdom of her plan. They were not flagrant doubts but tiny niggling pockets of uncertainty. She felt a little foolish.

She wanted to cry.

That was strange because Pip couldn't ever remember crying. What was even more peculiar was that she didn't know exactly why she felt so dejected. She couldn't recall feeling this way before. Nor could she ever remember such a feeling of incompetence . . . inadequacy . . . inferiority.

Shifting her position, Pip huddled with her arms around her bent legs and her chin propped on her knees. Why was it important what Sawyer Hayes thought? She stared, unseeing, out over the lake and tried to decipher these puzzling new emotions. With a quickness of mind and brilliance of logic that had dazzled others all her life, she sorted, categorized, then discarded thread after thread of possibilities. Until . . .

Inferiority!

Of course. *Industry versus inferiority* . . . late childhood . . . the time for learning skills, tasks, productivity, mastering the tools and fundamental technologies of society . . . evaluating oneself by comparison with peers. It was perfectly *normal* to experience these feelings of inferiority during this phase if she suspected that her accomplishments didn't compare favorably with those of others in her social environment.

Her plan *was* working. She needed to read more about Erikson's stage four of psychosocial development. Pip jumped up, and the boards of the pier rumbled under her feet as she bounded toward the house.

The two men stepped into the elevator that would take them from the helipad atop the Mirth Building, an imposing twenty-five-story glass structure in Houston's Greenway Plaza area, down one floor to the penthouse office of the company president. Sawyer, who rarely stood erect when he could lean, slouched against a teak wall of the private car and watched the door close with a faint whoosh.

Leonard pushed a button and said, "She's an odd duck. Who'd ever think that the famous Dr. Marguerite LeBaron would look like a kid?"

Sawyer didn't reply. He narrowed his eyes and chewed the inside of his lip until the door opened directly into the plush office. He sauntered over to a plump leather couch, sat down, and propped his feet on the glass coffee table.

"Do we still want her for the virtual reality project?" Leonard asked as he went to the bar and poured a drink.

Sawyer laced his hands over his stomach and stared at the steeple he'd made with his index fingers. "She's supposed to be the best in her field. Mirth always hires the best. But there may be some complications. She's determined not to take any jobs for several months."

Leonard snorted. "I can handle her. I've never met a woman yet who would turn down the right inducement—usually a pile of money."

"Uncle Len, I know your reputation for negotiation, but be careful with this one." Sawyer planted his feet on the thick carpet and stood. "She's special. Let me handle her."

He didn't explain to Len exactly how special he considered Pip. His uncle would go into apoplexy if he knew that Sawyer's plans for Pip had little to do with hiring her. He would rant and rave about his being besotted and sputter that chasing some woman was simply another of his harebrained schemes to avoid corporate responsibility. The tirades were becoming tiresome.

Sawyer repositioned his cap, walked over to his massive executive desk, and picked up the top letter on a stack his secretary had left for his signature. After scribbling his name on each of them, he took a folder from the top drawer and handed it to Leonard. "Take care of this first thing in the morning. I'll see you tomorrow. I've got to get to the library before it closes."

"The *library*?"

"Yep. I've got to do some reading. You know anything about theories of social development?"

"Good Lord, no. And why would you be interested?"

Sawyer hesitated, then grinned. Sooner or later Leonard was going to have to learn who was boss. "Dr. Pip."

Leonard Hooker frowned. "I hope you're not planning to go off on another of your wild escapades. It's time you settled down and took this business seriously. How do you think it looks to the board of directors—"

"Uncle Len," Sawyer interrupted, "lighten up." He strolled from the room whistling "Row, Row, Row Your Boat."

TWO

Pip clutched the heavy pot with her left hand and beat the thick chocolate mixture with the other. Her right arm was aching all the way up her shoulder, but she wielded the wooden spoon with the same intensity that she always devoted to projects. When she stopped to rest her arm and switch hands, she noticed that Sissy Strahan was sitting at the bar staring out the window, and her spoon lay idle in the crystallizing candy.

"Sissy, remember what Nan said. You have to beat like crazy to get the fudge creamy and firm."

A dreamy expression on her freckled face, the girl sighed, made a few halfhearted chops at the batch in her pot, and continued to stare out the window. "Wasn't he fine? Really fine? I think he's even cuter than Jason Priestley."

"Who is?"

"Sawyer."

Pip stopped her stirring, glanced up at the glassy-eyed preteen, and added her own small sigh. She had to agree. "Really fine."

After all, hadn't Sawyer Hayes been intruding on her thoughts all morning? At the oddest moments she would think of his intriguing face and his spectacular smile, and her throat would feel tight and her knees a little wobbly. It was the strangest thing, Pip thought. Her hand stilled, and she stared out the window with the same faraway look as Sissy, lost in her own visions of Sawyer. She was at a loss as to why he had affected her so, but he did.

"Good morning, ladies," a voice said from the doorway. "Nan told me I'd find you in here. Need any help?"

Pip looked up to see Sawyer Hayes leaning against the doorjamb, hands in the pockets of his jeans, grinning. What was he doing here? And what sort of inner joy did he possess that made him smile all the time?

It seemed incongruous to Pip that one person's smile should be so different from everyone else's, but Sawyer's was. The total infectiousness of it seemed to light the room and entreat all within its reach to join him in some secret mirth or joie de vivre. She wasn't immune.

Sissy's eyes brightened, and her smile widened around a mouthful of flashing silvery braces. "Hi, Sawyer. We were just talking about you."

Pip glanced at Sissy, who was fluttering her pale eyelashes, then back to Sawyer. He winked at Pip, and she felt her face go hot.

"You were, huh? Something good, I hope."

"Ohhh, it was," Sissy said.

Sawyer hadn't missed Pip's blush; he damn near popped his buttons with the idea that she might be half as interested in him as he was in her. He didn't miss much else about her either—not the shorts that cupped her cute little tush, the form-fitting T-shirt that showed a remarkable figure for one so small, nor the big, blue-purple-colored eyes with long black lashes. And her mouth. Mercy, what a mouth. It gave new meaning to the term *bee stung*, and it was made for kissing. She was even better than he remembered. With those funny glasses and the white blob on her nose gone, she was more than adorable. Dr. LeBaron was a pint-size knockout.

He sauntered toward Pip and peeked over her shoulder. Quickly he dipped a finger into the pot and popped the chocolate into his mouth. "Not bad, but it needs a little more beating."

Pip made a wry face. "I've beaten it until my hands are exhausted. It won't get hard."

Sawyer grinned as a bawdy thought flashed through his mind. Standing behind Pip, Sawyer reached around her, pinning her back against him as grabbed the pot and the spoon. "Here, let a pro give it a try."

After a few vigorous strokes, which brought Pip into intimate contact with his body, she wiggled and said, "Couldn't you do this better if I moved?"

"Uh-uh. You inspire me." That wasn't all she was doing to him. He was growing firmer than the fudge. "Where are the nuts?"

Sissy held up a cup of chopped pecans. "Right here."

"Dump 'em in," Sawyer said, still stirring briskly. He scanned the kitchen until he saw two lengths of waxed paper spread on the counter. He moved away before he embarrassed himself in front of the kid, and poured the candy on one strip of paper. With exaggerated brandishment he swirled the spoon over the mound. "Ah," he said, smacking the tips of his fingers in a noisy kiss, "fudge perfection. Want to lick the pot?" When Pip looked bewildered, he ran his finger around the inside until he had a nice-sized blob and held it an inch away from her lips.

She hesitated and looked up at him with those gorgeous eyes that made him want to free-fall into their depths.

He moved his finger closer, wishing it were his lips almost touching hers. "Go ahead. That's the best part."

Her tongue flicked out, and she took a tentative taste. "It's good."

"Told you. Have the rest." She hesitated again, and he knew she was uncomfortable. He could almost see the wheels turn in her pretty head. She opened her mouth and took his finger inside. The sucking sensation tightened his buttocks and tingled all the way down to his soles. He'd never guessed that fudge making could be such a turn-on.

"Oh, Sawyer, do mine. Do mine," Sissy said, breaking the intimacy of the moment.

Sawyer laughed and finished beating the girl's soupy batch. When the chocolate was poured and cut into squares, the three each grabbed a piece and declared it to be the very best fudge ever made.

Sissy heaved a theatrical sigh. "I have to go home now," she grumbled. "I'd rather stay here with y'all."

"We wish you could stay too," Pip said. "But you promised to be home by ten-thirty. You'd better hurry." She wrapped the girl's creation in foil for her to take along.

Sissy gave Sawyer a moon-eyed look and said a breathy, "Good-bye." However, her attempt at sophistication was spoiled when Sawyer grinned and winked at her. She blushed a deep scarlet, giggled, and ran out the door.

Pip knew exactly how Sissy felt, but she hoped her feelings weren't quite so obvious. Was this what an adolescent crush felt like? She didn't recall ever having felt this way as an adolescent.

Sawyer hoisted himself atop the counter and swung his legs while he gobbled another big piece of candy. "What are your plans for the rest of the day?"

"Since Sissy and Mark are going to visit their grandmother this weekend, I thought I'd build a birdhouse."

"A *birdhouse*?" He bit his lip to ward off laughter.

Pip drew herself erect and lifted her chin. "There is nothing amusing about building a birdhouse. It's on my list of activities appropriate for this developmental stage."

"I'm sure it is, Squirt. But we'll build it another day. There's somewhere I want to take you. You go powder your nose or whatever you have to do to get ready, and I'll tell Nan we're going out."

"Where are we going?"

"It's a surprise. Now, scoot," he said, giving her a swat on the fanny.

Pip decided to change into something less skimpy and settled on jeans, since that was what Sawyer was wearing. In fact, except for a clean shirt, she couldn't see any difference in his garb. She wondered where he was taking her. Usually she didn't care for surprises, but her skin fairly zinged with excitement.

When she joined him a few minutes later, his face fell visibly when she entered. Her heart lurched with dismay. She looked down at herself, then at him. "Is something wrong?"

"I was hoping you'd wear your shorts." He grinned slowly. "I like looking at your legs."

"You do?" His comment pleased her inordinately.

"You bettcha. You have *fine* legs."

"I do?"

"Haven't you ever looked in the mirror?"

"Of course, but they seem quite ordinary to me."

"Take my word for it, there's nothing ordinary about your legs—or the rest of you either. Don't tell me that nobody has clued you in."

"I don't recall anyone complimenting my legs before." Her quick mind, her problem-solving abilities, even her eyes occasionally, but never her legs. Of course she never wore shorts to work, and who could expect Uncle Waldo or Uncle Emory to notice such things? A warm, cozy feeling wiggled in the pit of her stomach. She discovered that she liked having Sawyer admire her legs. "Shall I change?"

"Naw, I'd probably be so distracted that I'd wrap the chopper around a radio tower. Come on, Short Stuff, let's burn daylight," he drawled, reaching for her hand.

"Are we going in the helicopter?"

"Right you are, Pilgrim," he drawled again, pulling her along as he started out the door, walking with a peculiar rolling gait.

"Did you injure your back?"

"No, why?"

"You seem to be walking in an odd way."

He threw back his head and laughed. "You sure know how to hurt a guy. That was my John Wayne imitation."

"Oh."

Drawing his brows together, he gave her a searching look. "You do know who John Wayne is, don't you?"

"Of course. I haven't been living on Mars. I've even seen *Pure Grit*."

Sawyer laughed. "That's *True Grit*, darlin'."

Embarrassed over her error, Pip mumbled, "Whatever."

His arm hooked around her neck, he drew her against him as he ambled toward the helipad. "Ah, Doctor, I can see that your education has some big gaps. I have my work cut out for me."

"I would appreciate it if you wouldn't address me as 'Doctor.' I only use the title professionally."

"I wasn't making fun of you. I admire that string of letters after your name. I never went to school myself."

"Surely you attended school somewhere."

"Nope. Not even kindergarten."

Horrified by his disclosure, Pip stopped

dead still. "But that's criminal. Where did you grow up?"

"In Houston. Oh, I had tutors, and I read a lot. I just never went to a regular school." They had reached the helicopter, and he opened the door to the small two-seater for her.

"Why ever not?"

"I'll tell you all about it sometime. Have you flown in one of these babies before?"

"Certainly. Many times. I find helicopters a very convenient means of travel in my profession. I even considered taking flying lessons once."

"Why didn't you?"

She shrugged. "For the same reason that I don't drive much. I decided that I wouldn't be a safe pilot. My mind tends to become engrossed with some problem I'm working on, and I get lost. Once, on my way home from NASA, I drove almost to Austin before I realized where I was." She cocked her head up at him and asked, "Has that ever happened to you?"

Sawyer looked down into her wide, guileless eyes, and something powerful stirred inside him. He understood being lost, all right; he was lost at that very moment. No more able to resist the temptation than he could cease to breathe, he bent and kissed her pert nose. "A couple of times."

Her huge pansy-colored eyes widened even farther, and she blinked several times as if surprised. He wanted to kiss her again—but for real this time. Not wanting to scare her off, he resisted the urge and helped her into the passenger seat.

When he'd settled behind the stick, he said in a mush-mouthed drawl, "Well, ah, Little Miss, ah, I guess we'd better be off."

She brightened. "John Wayne again, right?"

He laughed and shook his head. "Jimmy Stewart."

When the rotors died, Sawyer unbuckled his belt and ran around the chopper to help Pip out. "Where are we?" she asked, looking around. The truth was she'd been so preoccupied with watching Sawyer and thinking about the kiss on the nose he'd given her, that she hadn't the foggiest notion of the direction they'd taken. She'd finally decided that Sawyer was simply a casually demonstrative type and that his impulsive display was meaningless.

The conclusion left her with a nagging feeling of disappointment.

He made a sweeping gesture. "High atop the Mirth Building in Greenway Plaza." He offered his hand to assist her from the domed cockpit, then laced his fingers through hers and led her to the elevator.

"Why are we here?"

"I told you, it's a surprise." He used his keys to gain access to the elevator and pushed the fourth-floor button once they were inside.

When the door whooshed open, Sawyer stuck his head out and looked both ways before he stealthily pulled Pip behind him into the deserted, dimly lit hallway.

"Are you sure we should be here?" she whispered.

He grinned. Hearing footsteps around the corner, he hissed, "Cheese it, the guard," and yanked her into a recess beside a large potted plant.

Pip's heart beat furiously as she plastered herself against the wall, grabbed the stalk of the diffenbachia, and attempted to hide behind the leaves. She squeezed her eyes shut and tried not to breathe as she listened to the heavy footsteps becoming louder and louder.

Dear Lord, they were about to be nabbed

for trespassing. Never in her life had she done anything untoward; no hint of scandal or impropriety had ever touched her name. Now she had visions of being hauled off to jail and the event headlined in the *Houston Chronicle*. Her security clearance at NASA, her standing with the university, her reputation in the business community would be in jeopardy.

The steps halted directly in front of their hiding place, which was, Pip thought, skimpy at best. The hair on the back of her neck prickled, and her heart felt as if it had stopped completely. She kept her eyes closed and a death grip on the stalk.

"Oh, Sawyer, it's you," a deep voice said.

"How's it going, Hank?"

"Can't complain."

One of her eyes opened, then the other as Sawyer said to the guard, "I was just showing Dr. LeBaron around the place. She's fond of plants."

Pip released the stalk, and the plant sprang back into its upright position, leaves aquiver.

The guard touched the bill of his cap. "Ma'am."

She nodded, and Hank moved on. She didn't budge until she heard the elevator door close. Sawyer looked as if he might explode with laughter. She balled up her fist and smacked him on the shoulder. "You stinker!"

His laughter burst its restraints. "I had you going there for a minute, didn't I?" He tugged her long pigtail.

She whopped him again. "You unspeakable rat! You almost frightened me to death."

Still laughing, he took off down the hall with Pip running after him, shouting deprecations and threatening bodily harm. He stopped in front of a double door and let her overtake him. Catching her up by the waist, he whirled her around, then stopped and looked down at her.

Merriment crinkled the corners of his eyes and skipped from their sparkling-green depths. His lips looked as if they could barely contain the laughter that lifted their outer limits. A chuckle made its way up her own throat, then another and another.

They were both laughing then, and he swung her around again.

"I love the sound of your laughter," he said. "It's like silver bells on a dewy morning. You should do it more often." He set her down and kissed the tip of her nose.

He turned to unlock the double doors, and Pip, still smiling, touched her nose where the sensation of his kiss lingered like a warm shadow. The doors open, he turned back around, and she quickly pulled her hand away.

He bowed and swept his arm in a broad flourish. "After you."

"Are you sure we should be here?"

With a bobble of his head he said smugly, "The boss and I are like that." He held up crossed fingers. "Trust me."

She scanned the large room that they entered, and she quickly defined it as a technical laboratory complete with the latest and most sophisticated computers. He led her to a table and picked up a pair of gloves interwoven with a myriad of small multicolored wires and a pair of oversized goggles.

"Recognize these?" he asked.

She briefly studied the computer-connected gloves and the goggles. "I assume that they are a part of some virtual reality venture. I've worked on several projects for NASA, usually flight simulation and that sort of thing." She examined the goggles, which were fitted with tiny television screens. "These are an excellent design. Very sleek, very compact. What is their purpose?"

"You'll see. Come on."

When he tried to position her in one of two squares outlined with blue tape on the floor, she balked. "I need an explanation first."

"It's my surprise. You'll get a kick out of it."

She looked at the blue squares, which were separated by a smaller red one, the gloves, the goggles, the computers. She felt a terrible aching in her chest, and her eyes narrowed. "Is this"—she made a sweeping gesture around the room—"are *you*"—she glared at him—"part of some elaborate strategy to engage my professional services?"

Sawyer's smile slowly died, and a stricken look crept over his features. "No." He shook his head and held up his right hand, palm out. "Swear to God. I only wanted to surprise you. Whether or not you go to work for Mirth has nothing to do with this."

The ache in her chest abated, and she smiled. "Well, then, what's the surprise?"

"You'll see. Put these on." He handed her the gloves and goggles with built-in earpieces for audio. "Stand here." He again positioned her in one of the squares and picked up a baseball bat. "We're going to do a little batting practice. How about Nolan Ryan?"

"Who's Nolan Ryan?"

Sawyer shook his head. "One of the greatest pitchers of all time. Do you have an idea of what we're doing here?"

"From your comments and from the pressure-sensitive gloves and the other virtual reality paraphernalia, I assume that it's some sort of simulated baseball game." She pointed to the squares. "The blue ones must be batters' boxes and the red one in the middle is home plate."

"Bright lady."

She shrugged. "Simple deduction."

"Want to try it?"

"It would be interesting."

Sawyer turned on the computer, placed her in the batter's box, and helped her on with the gear. He handed her the bat. "Find your comfortable stance, and we'll start out slowly. I'll cut down the speed on Ryan's fast ball and give you strikes right over the plate. All you have to do is keep your eye on the ball and swing at it. Okay?"

"Okay."

"Ready?"

"Ready."

Suddenly Pip was on a baseball field, facing a pitcher as he wound up to throw. The next thing she knew, she heard the thwack of a ball in a mitt, and a gruff voice yelled, "Strike!"

"Too fast?" Sawyer asked.

"I wasn't prepared."

"I'll slow it down a little more."

The pitcher wound up again, and Pip swung at the ball as it sailed past.

"Strike!"

Another pitch. Another swing. Through the pressure simulation of the gloves she felt the bat connect with the image of a ball and heard the loud crack as they met.

"Pop fly," the computer voice said. "Foul ball." The voice proceeded to give instructions for a change of stance and a repositioning of her hands for optimum results.

She adjusted according to directions. After a few more pitches and a few more adjustments, her bat connected with a good solid hit. She could feel it through the gloves before the computer's voice announced, "Line drive!"

Throwing down the bat, Pip ripped off the goggles and squealed, "Did you see that? I did it!"

Sawyer laughed. "You sure did. Want to try it again?"

"You bet!"

After several more hits Pip called a halt.

"I'd better quit while I'm ahead." Excitement bubbled inside her. "I love this. It's fantastic. Is it on the market yet?"

"Not yet—and I don't have to tell you that it's top secret. But this thing is the hottest invention ever for simulated batting practice. It'll be available in a few months for college and pro teams. And in about another year for the younger kids. It's a great tool for Little League practice, too, but a few kinks have to be worked out first. Mirth is also working on a 'Virtual Reality for Golfers.' "

"Sounds fascinating. Is this the project Mr. Hooker wanted me to work on?"

"Think so. Say, how about some lunch? What sounds good?" He laced his fingers with hers and pulled her toward the door. "How about enchiladas? I've got a yen for Mexican food."

"Sounds great. Are we going to take the helicopter?"

"Naw, I've got a car downstairs in the garage."

Pip ordered chicken fajitas in perfect Spanish. When the waiter left, Sawyer said, "I'm impressed."

"Why?"

"My Spanish vocabulary is limited to *munchin' grasses*."

Pip giggled. "I think your pronunciation could use some improvement too. I think that's *muchas gracias*."

He grinned, tickled to be able to make her laugh. "Never could trill those *r*s. My tongue gets all tangled up. I'll bet you're one of those people who speak two or three languages. Right?"

She shrugged and dug into the tortilla chips and salsa. "Four fluently. And a little of a couple of others. What language did you study?"

"English. I've gotten pretty good at it, if I do say so myself."

She giggled again. Lord, he loved the sound of it. Like tiny Christmas bells. And the way her eyes lit up warmed him all over and melted his heart as if it were candle wax. He was thoroughly and completely besotted. Captivated by Dr. Pip LeBaron's perky nose and pansy eyes.

And her lips.

And her legs.

And everything about her.

She leaned forward and said conspiratorially, "Sounds like you have a few gaps in your education."

Delighted by her teasing, his grin widened as he dipped into the salsa. "Yep. One or two. Say, do you speak French?"

She nodded. "And German. My Arabic and Russian are only passable."

"I've always wanted to learn French. I'll make you a deal. You teach me how to speak French, and I'll teach you how to play and have fun. Deal?" He struck out his hand.

"Deal." She took his hand.

He didn't want to let it go. He wanted to hang on to her forever. Being with Pip made him feel as if someone had blown up a balloon inside his chest. He wanted to stand on the table and crow.

Instead he sat there grinning like a fool.

An idea popped into his head, and he tugged her hand. "Come on, I want to take you somewhere with me."

"Aren't we going to eat first?"

He laughed and scooted back into the booth. "Oh, yeah. I forgot."

"Where did you want to take me?"

"It's another surprise. Do you like horses?"

She looked pensive for a moment. "I really don't know."

"You don't know? Do you mean that you grew up in Texas and you've never ridden a horse?"

"Sorry. Do you think the governor will revoke my citizenship?"

His features schooled into a solemn expression, he stroked his chin. "She might. I suppose I could teach you if the price was right."

"I thought we already had a deal."

"Mmmm. But this is something extra I hadn't counted on."

She cocked her head in a charming way that almost undid him. "What is the price?"

"Ohhh," he said, acting as if he had to give the matter some thought. "How about a kiss?"

She blinked her long eyelashes twice, three times. "Sounds fair."

Sawyer was only vaguely aware of the waiter serving their food. He watched Pip's dainty fingers prepare a fajita; he sat enthralled as she took a bite. A tiny spot of sour cream at the corner of her mouth captured his attention. When her tongue flicked out and retrieved it, he was disappointed. His fantasy called for his tongue to lick it away.

Imagining his lips on hers, Sawyer wasn't sure whether he was eating enchiladas or wood shavings.

THREE

Pip looked around as Sawyer helped her from the helicopter. "Where are we?"

"At Mirth Ranch," he said.

"The corporation owns a ranch?"

"Sort of."

She frowned. "I've never asked, but exactly what kind of a company is Mirth?"

Sawyer ran his fingers through his hair and repositioned his green cap. "Mirth's involved in lots of things—all concerned with entertainment, sports, and leisure activities. They have some retail outlets, but mostly they develop and manufacture toys and games, sports equipment, stuff like that."

"I see. Why the ranch?"

Before he could answer, a miniature tornado with a face full of freckles and a mop of carrot-colored curls charged toward them yelling, "Sawyer! Sawyer!"

"Hey, Scooter," Sawyer said.

The little boy, dressed in jeans and boots, opened his arms and launched himself at Sawyer, who squatted and caught the child in a big hug before they toppled together in the grass, laughing.

After a moment of tussling and tickling, Sawyer stood and pulled the child to his feet. The boy grinned broadly and pointed to a large gap in his teeth.

"What's this I see?" Sawyer asked. "Lose another one, Scooter?"

Scooter puffed out his thin chest. "Yep. And I put it under my pillow like you said, and I found a quarter there the next morning."

"Told you that tooth fairy was on the ball." Sawyer drew Pip close to him and said to her, "This is one of my pardners, Scooter Wiggins. Scooter, this is Doctor Pip."

Pip smiled at the child, whom she judged to be about six years old. He suddenly turned shy, wrapped his arms around Sawyer's leg, and peeked at her from behind Sawyer's thigh. "She's a *girl*," he whispered.

"Yep," Sawyer said. "I noticed that right off too."

"Does she give shots?"

"Nope. She's not that kind of doctor. She's a scientist doctor. Sometimes she works with the astronauts."

"She *does*?" Scooter's big brown eyes grew wide. He stepped from his hiding place and looked Pip over carefully. "Have you ever been in a spaceship?"

"A few times."

"Have you ever been to the *moon*?"

Smiling, Pip shook her head. "Afraid not. I've only been in the spaceships when they were on the ground. But I've worked with some of the astronauts who have been in space."

"You *have*?" Scooter's eyes grew wider. "I'm gonna be a asternot when I grow up."

"I thought you were going to be a rodeo cowboy and ride wild bulls," Sawyer said.

"I am. Gonna be a asternot *and* ride bulls. Big, mean ones. And I'm gonna fly a helicopter too." He beamed up at Sawyer, hero worship evident in his eyes.

Sawyer ruffled his hair. "Say, Sport, where is everybody?"

Scooter kicked at a clump of Johnson grass with the toe of his boot. "Most everybody's gone to the movies. Everybody but me and Davy and Mister Matt."

"Why didn't you and Davy go?"

Scooter looked down and mumbled.

"I didn't hear that."

"It was on account of Walter and Mister Matt's 'lectric razor." The boy glanced up at Sawyer, a stricken expression on his face. "We only done it 'cause Walter kept gettin' cockleburs so bad. Even Mister Matt says it's a son-of-a-gun gettin' all them burrs out. Me and Davy thought up a great idea."

Amusement danced in his eyes as Sawyer said to Pip, "Walter is one of the ranch dogs. A collie mix. It's part of the boys' responsibility to help take care of the animals." To Scooter he said, "I take it that you and Davy shaved Walter with Mister Matt's razor."

"Uh-huh. But not all over. Just the part with the burrs. But Mister Matt got all red in the face, and Miz Mary said we couldn't go to the movies and to go to our room and think about what we done. Me and Davy thinked and thinked. We thinked real hard. Davy thinked so hard he went to sleep, but I didn't. I heard your helicopter, and here I am." He gave Sawyer an engaging, snaggle-toothed grin.

Pip bit her lip to keep from laughing, and

Sawyer seemed to be having the same trouble. "I hope you learned a lesson," Sawyer said.

Scooter nodded. "Don't shave a dog with someone else's propity."

"Property?"

"Mister Matt's razor."

"I see."

"You ain't mad at me?"

"Nope."

Pip saw Scooter's thin shoulders sag. "You ain't gonna whip me with your belt?"

"Nope. That's not the way we do things around here. You know that."

Scooter's eyes brightened. "I told Davy wadn't nobody gonna whip us, but he was scared."

Sawyer hugged the boy and gave him a gentle push. "You run tell Mister Matt that I'm here with a guest to go riding. Okay?"

" 'Kay." Scooter took off toward one of two large white ranch houses near a cluster of cottages and a big red barn.

The exchange between boy and man had evoked a sweet sentiment unusual in Pip's experience. The warmth and affection evident between them had produced a lump in her throat and a soft glow in her heart. "He's adorable," she said, watching the boy's short legs churn toward his destination. "And so outgoing."

"He's come a long way in the six months he's been here. He cowered like a whipped dog when he first came."

Puzzled, she said, "I don't understand."

He threw an arm around her shoulders and led her in the direction Scooter had gone. "He was badly abused at home. All the kids here were abused in one way or another."

"All?"

He nodded. "We usually have about a dozen or so boys between six and twelve. Matt Emerson and his wife, Mary, manage the place. He's sort of the ranch foreman, and she runs the kitchen. We have two sets of house parents, a child psychologist, and a couple of ranch hands. Two ladies come in to help with the cleaning, cooking, and laundry." He grinned. "There's *lots* of cooking and laundry with that many boys."

Pip laughed. "I can imagine. Mirth sponsors the program?"

"Yep."

"And you obviously spend a great deal of time here. How commendable of both you and the company."

Sawyer shrugged and seemed embarrassed.

"It's not enough." He waved to a wiry, gray-haired man who appeared on the porch of one of the ranch houses. "Hey, Matt."

When they approached, Sawyer introduced Pip to the foreman just as Scooter and a tousled-haired towhead ran out the front door. The second boy launched himself into Sawyer's arms, much as Scooter had done, and clung to his neck.

"Hey, there, Davy," Sawyer said. "I hear you and Scooter got into a little trouble." Davy burrowed his head closer into the crook of Sawyer's shoulder. "Learned your lesson?"

Not lifting his head, Davy nodded.

"Ruined my danged razor," Matt said. "They had to forfeit movies and pizza to pay for it."

"Did you apologize to Mister Matt, Davy?"

Davy shook his head.

"I did," Scooter piped up.

"Why don't you apologize now?" Sawyer asked Davy.

The boy scrunched closer to Sawyer and looked at Matt. Matt waited.

Davy held out his arms to Matt. The wiry old man reached for him and hugged him. Davy kissed his leathered cheek, and tears misted Pip's eyes as she watched the crusty Matt swipe at his nose.

"Davy, this is Doctor Pip. I'm going to teach her how to ride a horse. You and Scooter want to come along and help?" When Davy eyed her carefully and nodded, Sawyer said to Pip, "Davy doesn't talk much yet."

" 'Cept to me," Scooter said. "He talks to me."

Sawyer laughed. "How can he get a word in edgewise? I'm going out to saddle up a couple of mounts. Why don't you boys take Doctor Pip to the corral?"

"Okey dokey," Scooter said and grabbed Pip's hand. Davy timidly clasped the other, and they pulled her along after them.

At the corral the boys scampered up the fence and straddled the top rail. Davy sat solemnly while Scooter chattered about whatever popped into his head. When he saw Sawyer and another man leading two horses and two ponies, he said, "Wow, look, Davy. We're going to get to ride. I'm sure glad Sawyer didn't get mad at us for being bad."

"Oh, I don't think you were bad," Pip said. "I think you simply made an error in judgment."

"A what?"

"An error in judgment. A mistake. Everybody makes mistakes now and then. The secret is to learn from our mistakes and not repeat them."

"You hear that, Davy? We wasn't bad. We made errs in—" He frowned at Pip.

"Judgment."

"We made errs in judgment. Do asternots ever make errs in judgment?"

"Not often, but sometimes. They're very careful not to make mistakes because their errors could have serious ramifications."

Scooter frowned. "What's ram—?"

"Ramifications?"

"Yeah, what you said."

"It's everything that could happen as a result of their mistake. All sorts of things could go wrong."

"Like if they pushed the wrong button, they could go to Mars instead of the moon?"

Pip chuckled. "Yes, something like that."

"Wow!"

Sawyer grinned as he approached Pip and the two boys. "Are you guys plotting something?"

"Nope," Scooter said. "We're talking about errs in judgment. Did you know that we wasn't bad when we shaved Walter? We made an err in judgment. Even asternots make errs in judgment, 'n' they have serious ramercations— like goin' to Mars and not gettin' to go to the movies."

Sawyer cocked an eyebrow. "Want to run that by me again?"

"I was explaining cause and effect," Pip said. "Errors in judgment and ramifications."

"I see."

She smiled. "You had to have been there. I think they got the gist of the principle."

He opened the gate for her and showed her the two gentle mares from the stable. "We have here Blossom and Fancy. Which one would you like to ride?"

"I have no preference. Why don't you decide?"

"Let's try you on Blossom."

"I have no idea how to begin."

"Grab the saddle horn, put your left foot here," Sawyer said, holding the stirrup, "and swing your right leg over the saddle."

She gamely tried to do as he instructed, but she hopped around trying to mount, and the horse shifted impatiently. Finally Sawyer boosted her up with a palm to her backside. The stirrups were a bit too long, and Pip clung to the horn with both hands. She looked decidedly nervous.

"I think she's kinda scared," Scooter offered in a stage whisper. "Why don't you teach her to ride the way you did Davy and me?"

"Good idea," Sawyer replied, trying to keep the amusement from his voice. "Move forward in the saddle," he told Pip.

He swung up behind her and instantly realized that he had a problem. That cute little fanny with jeans stretched tightly over her curves was like fire between his legs. He tried to move back, but the dip of the saddle insisted on intimate contact.

Reaching around her to gather the reins, his cheek brushed the tendrils of hair on her temples. Smelling of sunshine and flowers, the dark wisps were silky soft against his skin. He let his cheek linger there and whispered, "Relax against me. I won't let you fall."

"Promise?"

"Promise. We'll just walk around the corral a couple of times for you to get used to the feel." *The feel of* me *and the feel of the horse*, he thought.

As her weight relaxed along the front of his body, his breath caught. Her delicate contours molded against his as if she were made for him. She *was* made for him. Gently he urged the mare forward.

With Blossom's every plodding step, leather creaked, and Pip's bottom rubbed against the juncture of his thighs. His pulse quickened and his heart almost hammered through his chest. He squirmed and found no relief; with the shape of the saddle, her body followed his. Every point of contact, even the area where his arms touched hers, was magnified until he was filled with tactile awareness and oblivious to everything but Pip and the feel of her.

The sun warmed her scent, and it rose to his nostrils, tantalizing, teasing, until his senses were bursting with her.

She laughed, and the sound of it poured over him like a warm shower.

"You like this?" he asked, the sound of his own voice strange to him. He cleared his throat.

"Yes." Her voice sounded as husky as his. "It's very . . ."

"Very . . . ?"

"Uh . . . uh . . . strange. Different."

She ducked her head and tried to scoot forward. He filled the small space she'd vacated, and they were molded closely again.

He bent his head and nuzzled the side of her neck. "I thought you were going to say 'erotic.' "

She cleared her throat. "That too."

A series of whistles and laughter came from the fence. Startled, they both glanced over to find a dozen boys watching them. He felt her stiffen.

"Oh, dear. Maybe we'd better get off."

"Maybe you'd better get off. I don't think I should right now."

"Why ever not?"

"Because . . . well, let's just say that being this close to you plays hell with my libido, and my jeans are pretty tight at the moment."

Pip giggled.

He grinned. "My saying that didn't shock you?"

"Shock me? Why, good heavens, no. I don't shock easily. I'm a very modern woman."

His hunch was that she wasn't being exactly truthful. Her back was a little too straight, and her words seemed delivered with a stilted bravado. He would have bet both his record and CD collections that her face was flaming. In a era where blushing had become a lost art, she blushed beautifully. It made him wonder exactly how sexually experienced she was. Not very, he guessed.

The idea pleased the hell out of him. He'd

been a late bloomer himself. Of course once initiated, he'd made up for lost time. He'd never suffered a lack of female companionship. But of all the women he'd known, he'd never found the one who ignited that certain spark of magic inside.

Until Pip.

"What are we going to do?" she asked.

If they did what he wanted to do, they would ride off into the sunset—or at least far away from a dozen impressionable boys who were watching their every move.

"If I ride close to the fence, can you climb off?"

"I'll try."

The feat was easily accomplished. Sawyer rode Blossom to where Bill, one of the hands, stood patiently holding the other mare and the two ponies.

"Bill, would you supervise some of the boys on the horses for a while? I'm going to ride Blossom into the barn."

Bill answered with a knowing grin and a tug of his cowboy hat. "She's a right pretty little filly, Sawyer. Enough to get a man's blood stirring."

Sawyer laughed and kicked the mare's sides. His blood was stirring for sure.

❧━━━━◆━━━━❧

As Pip watched Sawyer ride the horse back to the barn, she felt a peculiar quickening in her body. She seemed to glow from the inside out. Her respiration was rapid. Her heartbeat soared well above its usual rate. She felt herself smiling for no particular reason.

Odd. Very odd.

Was this what falling in love did to a person?

Falling in love?

She hadn't been acquainted with Sawyer long enough to fall in love. Perhaps she was forming a mild infatuation. But then she had no experience on which to base a comparison. She'd never been infatuated. Nor in love.

She'd never even been in lust. Not really. Her encounters with men had been primarily platonic—dinners with colleagues, occasional concerts with friends, and such. Only once or twice had her engagements with men produced more than a casual kiss on the cheek or a handshake at the end of the evening. She'd found those exceptions—wet kisses and unpleasant groping—distasteful, if not totally disgusting. Certainly there was nothing romantic about them.

Not that she was completely naive about sexual relationships. She'd read extensively on the subject. Everything from the elementary mating habits of simple-celled creatures to the more complex ones of *Homo sapiens*. None of the feelings and behaviors had seemed relevant to her.

She had assumed that society's preoccupation with sexuality and romance was grossly exaggerated, an idea perpetuated by ad agencies and sentimental women's fiction. Either that or something was missing in her hormonal makeup.

Or her personality.

Perhaps that had been the case, she surmised—another of the gaps in her social development.

When she'd first reached adolescence, she'd already been in college. And college men weren't interested in a thirteen- or fourteen-year-old girl. Especially one who looked even younger. She'd never had the opportunity to interact with boys her own age. There had been no proms, no parties, no dates to the movies.

Study and work had become the focus of her life.

But something strange was happening to her now.

Sawyer Hayes had unlocked a door, and dormant female hormones had awakened with a frenzy. The feeling of his body so close to hers in the saddle was definitely . . . erotic.

It was puzzling.

It was exciting.

It was frightening.

But she liked it.

She needed to do considerably more research into the matter. First thing tomorrow she'd go to the university library.

When Sawyer walked from the barn, smiling as he approached, thoughts of research and libraries fled. All she wanted to do was touch him.

FOUR

Before he could reach her, Sawyer was surrounded by the dozen youngsters, all vying for his attention. He took the time to speak to each one, laughing, exchanging a playful poke or a hug.

When he finally made it to the fence rail where Pip sat waiting for him, his smile brightened and his eyes sparkled with a devilish glint. "I'm afraid you didn't get much instruction today in horseback riding. We'll come back next week when the kids are in school. Okay?"

"Mais oui!"

He reached up and lifted her down from the fence. "No problem. We won't be disrupting anything."

"Not 'may we.' I said, *'mais oui.'* It's sort of the French equivalent for 'for sure' or 'sure enough.' Literally *mais* means *but*, and *oui* means *yes*. It's your first French lesson. Got it?"

He winked and swaggered his head. *"Mais oui!"*

A few minutes later Pip and Sawyer waved good-bye to the boys who had followed them to the helipad. *"Au revoir,"* Sawyer called to the kids. To Pip he said, "I learned that in an old Charles Boyer movie. Did I say it right?" He squeezed her hand.

"Perfect. They're all very fond of you," she said as he helped her into the passenger seat.

"I'm fond of them too. They're good kids who've had some bad breaks. I like to spend as much time with them as I can."

"Is your employer as involved with the boys as you are?"

"My employer? You mean Leonard Hooker? He's not my employer. He only thinks he is sometimes. And no, he's not interested in Mirth Ranch at all. In fact if he had his way, he'd shut down the place. It cuts into the corporation's profit margin."

Aghast, Pip said, "But you can't let him *do* that!"

Sawyer smiled and rubbed his nose against hers. "I knew you were my kind of woman. And don't worry. As long as I'm the boss, it won't happen."

She frowned. "As long as *you're* the boss?"

"Yep. I'm the major stockholder in Mirth. The company's my baby."

She eyed him suspiciously. "I think you have some explaining to do."

He only grinned and started the engine. "Later," he shouted over the sound of the rotors.

The last glow of the sun was settling behind the tall pine trees when Sawyer walked Pip to the porch of the lake house. Her fingers threaded through his felt as delicate and fragile as fine porcelain, yet warm.

Incredibly warm. Electrically warm.

And soft.

He had to remind himself not to squeeze too hard, for he wanted nothing more than to hold on to her forever.

The air seemed sweeter, the breeze off the

lake seemed crisper, his step seemed lighter with her at his side. All day an ache to hold her close and kiss her had grown stronger and stronger. So potent was the ache that it filled his entire awareness.

When they reached the door, she looked up at him with those big, beautiful eyes, and he wanted to wade into their hypnotic brilliance. He wanted to tuck her beneath his arm and fly with her beyond the setting sun. He wanted . . .

He wanted . . .

He gently touched her cheek, his fingertips savoring skin as silken as a butterfly's wing. He brushed at the tendrils around her face, and one curled around his finger like a playful sprite. Teasing, tempting, tantalizing.

"I suppose I must say *bonne nuit*," she murmured.

So engrossed was he with drinking in her presence that her words barely registered. *"Bonne nuit?"*

"Good night. It's been a lovely day. *Merci beaucoup*. Thank you very much."

"The pleasure has been all mine. And tomorrow we'll have another lovely day. But first"—he traced the outline of her lips—"I must do something I've wanted to do all day.

Something I've wanted to do since the first time I saw you."

Her eyes widened, and she blinked her long, lush lashes. "And what . . . what is that?"

"I'd like to kiss you. Do you mind?"

Her lids flickered, and she said a breathy, *"Non."*

When his lips touched hers, Pip melted like a snowflake on a summer day. His mouth was soft and warm and delicious. The sun seemed to burst forth behind her closed eyelids, and exquisite ripples of sensation spread over her entire body. She wanted the feeling to go on and on. But he pulled away.

He blew out a soundless whistle. "I think I'd better say *bonne nuit*."

Her heart sank. "You didn't like kissing me?"

"Oh, I liked kissing you. A lot."

She smiled. "I liked it too. Must you go? Would you like to stay for dinner? I'm sure Nan has plenty fixed. Saturday is usually spaghetti night. Do you like spaghetti?"

"I adore spaghetti."

"Then you'll stay?"

"Mais oui!"

Inside, they headed for the kitchen with Pip calling, "Nan, I'm home."

The gray-haired lady, who looked like a bricklayer with bangs, glanced up from the pot she stirred. " 'Bout time. I was getting worried."

Pip laughed and kissed the housekeeper's cheek. "Nan, will you ever stop worrying about me? I'm a grown woman."

Sawyer hoisted himself onto the counter by the stove, then broke off a piece of garlic bread and dipped it into the bubbling sauce. "Ummm, heaven, Nan." He took another bite. "Ummm, that's good stuff." He screwed his face into an expression of absolute ecstasy and kissed the tips of his fingers. "Wonderful. Better than my mother's. Nan, you're a genius in the kitchen." He gave her an engaging grin and sat on the counter swinging his legs. "Will you marry me?"

"Aw, go on, you rascal." Nan stood taller, and a dimple appeared in her cheek as she pursed her lips trying hard to mask her feelings. It was obvious that the woman couldn't have been more pleased if she'd been awarded a Nobel Prize. Sawyer Hayes charmed her the same way he charmed everyone around him.

"I invited Sawyer to stay for dinner," Pip said. "I knew you'd have enough."

"Always plenty of food at my table." Over

the top of her gold-rimmed glasses, Nan looked Sawyer's trim frame up and down. "You look like you could use some extra meat on your bones too. Half the time this one"—she gestured with her head toward Pip—"doesn't eat enough to keep a bird alive. Gets some highfalutin' notion in her head and forgets all about food. Body's got to have three square meals a day, I always say. I'm partial to hearty eaters."

"That's me," Sawyer said.

"Oh, Nan, if I ate everything you wanted me to, I'd be a butterball."

"Humph. Dinner will be ready in about thirty minutes. I'll set the table out on the screened porch. It's right cozy and nice out there this time of year."

"Need any help?" Sawyer asked.

"You'd just get in my way. Why don't the two of you take a nice brisk walk and work up a good appetite?"

After Nan shooed them from the kitchen, Sawyer grinned down at Pip. "Want to take a nice brisk walk?"

"No, but I would like to freshen up a bit. I smell of horse. You can use the guest bath if you'd like."

His eyes crinkled with amusement. "Are you insinuating that I reek of *eau de* horse?"

She laughed. "*Cheval*. Not at all. I like the way—" She stopped before she finished the sentence and ducked her head. Unsure of the social nuances between men and women, she didn't want to say the wrong thing and make a fool of herself. Ordinarily she was an open and direct communicator, not used to censoring her words.

He lifted her chin. "You like the way—what?"

She bit her lip, then blurted out, "I like the way you smell."

A slow grin spread over his face. "And how do I smell?"

Cocking her head, she said, "I'm not sure that I can describe it exactly."

He kissed her lightly on the lips. "You smell like sunshine and flowers."

"I do?"

"Um-hmmm."

"How lovely. I'm afraid I'm not very poetic."

"Me either." He pressed his forehead to hers. "Maybe we can learn together."

Pip felt as if she were trying to navigate in zero gravity as she walked to her room. She felt muzzy-headed, and her body seemed so light, so buoyant, that her feet hardly touched the floor. And her thoughts didn't seem as sharp and well defined as usual.

The strange thing was that she didn't care. The remnants of Sawyer's aura wrapped her in a cuddly cocoon and penetrated her whole being. She hugged herself trying to draw it closer.

Ridiculous of course. There was nothing tangible to draw closer.

Still she felt something almost palpable.

In the bathroom she squinted at herself in the mirror. Except for a smudge on her chin, she didn't look any different. But in the short time since Sawyer had flown into her life, she felt different.

Very different.

She touched her lips where he'd kissed her, remembering, savoring the feeling. And fervently hoping he'd kiss her again.

After washing up and making a few repairs, she went to the living room. Sawyer stood by a bookshelf, looking at a collection of framed photographs. He picked one up.

"This looks like Alice in Wonderland with Tweedledum and Tweedledee."

Pip chuckled. "Hardly. Those are my uncles, and I'm in the middle. It was taken in Paris when I was about ten. Uncle Waldo and Uncle Emory taught for a year in France as part of a university exchange program, and I went with them. I had a glorious time."

"That where you learned French?"

"Yes. I had a wonderful tutor there."

Sawyer peered closely at the picture. "You're cute in your pinafore, but which uncle is which? They look exactly alike."

"They're identical twins. That's Uncle Emory on the left. They still look exactly alike, except that now they're a little plumper, a little grayer, and a little more bald. They're both sweethearts." She sniffed the tantalizing scent of spaghetti sauce and garlic bread and discovered that she was famished. "Let's see if dinner's ready. Are you hungry?"

Sawyer rubbed his stomach. "I think I could eat old Blossom if you put some butter on her."

She laughed, and he hooked his arm around her neck and drew her to him for a small peck on the nose.

"I love to hear you laugh. You need to laugh more. Have I told you that?"

She nodded. "It's easy to laugh with you."

When they arrived on the porch, Pip found a small table set for two, complete with flickering candles, a hastily arranged container of flowers, and wineglasses. As Nan bustled in with a steaming platter of spaghetti and meat-balls, Pip looked askance at her.

"Where is your place, Nan?"

"Oh, I'm going to eat on a TV tray in my room. It's almost time for that police story I like to watch on Channel Thirteen."

"Police story?"

"Yes, police story," Nan said brusquely. "Now, you two enjoy your dinner and don't worry about the dishes. I'll tend to them later."

After the housekeeper set down the platter and hurried from the room, Pip leaned across the table and whispered, "Nan hates TV. What do you suppose is wrong with her?"

Sawyer grinned. "I imagine she's trying to promote a romantic evening for just the two of us. Reckon this means she likes me?"

"Obviously."

"I think you should give her a raise. Shall I pour the wine?"

Never had spaghetti tasted so delicious. And Pip had two—or was it three?—glasses of wine beyond her usual limit of one. The candle flames seemed to dance on the tips of the wicks while the night creatures around the lake provided music. Honeysuckle growing over an arbor near the porch filled the air with sweet scents as she and Sawyer talked of inconsequential things and simply enjoyed each other's company.

Was this a part of life that she'd been missing? How sad, she thought, for she found it extremely satisfying. Perhaps it was Sawyer who made the difference. She liked being with him. He made her feel lighthearted and carefree.

She wanted to laugh, fling out her arms, and dance.

"But I can't dance," she muttered.

"Pardon?"

She heaved a big sigh. "I can't dance."

"That's easy to remedy. I'll teach you."

She brightened. "You will?"

"*Mais oui!* I'm a dancing fool. Got any records?"

"In the living room." She rose too quickly, and her head spun. "Oops." She giggled and plopped back down in her chair. "I think I had too much wine. I never drink more than one glass."

"You killed over half the bottle."

"No, I couldn't have."

He upended the empty bottle. "But you did."

She leaned across the table and whispered conspiratorially, "I think I drank too much because I was nervous."

"Nervous? Why?"

"I was thinking about you kissing me again. Have you thought about it too?"

"It's been on my mind."

Suddenly she grew very warm. "Let's see about the records." Rising quickly, she struck out for the living room.

Sawyer followed her. Tipsy, Dr. Pip LeBaron was about the most adorable thing he'd ever seen. Her cute little tush seemed to swing with a sexy twitch that—*Careful*, he told himself. *Slow and easy does it.*

"Here are the records I have." She pointed to a stack on a shelf. "Perhaps you can find something appropriate."

He sorted through the stack, then laughed. "Rachmaninoff's stuff has a nice beat, but you can't dance to it."

Pip blinked her eyes, looking endearingly blank.

He wrapped his arms around her waist and smiled down at her. "Nothing in your collection is appropriate. But don't worry about it. Tomorrow we'll go to my place. I've got hundreds of records we can dance to."

"What shall we do in the meantime?"

He grinned. "Wanna go frog giggin'?"

"What does it entail?"

Laughing, he shook his head. "I was teasing. Let's go sit on the porch swing and count lightning bugs. Ever done that?"

"I don't believe that I have."

Outside, the chain creaked as the swing took their weight. Pip drew her feet under her, and Sawyer moved close, placing his arm around her and snuggling her against him.

Hundreds of fireflies seemed to hover and flicker over the dew-dampened grass.

"Pretty, aren't they?" Sawyer asked. "Like tiny winking fairy lanterns."

"Actually," Pip said, enunciating her words carefully, "the intermittent luminescence is a result of the oxidation of luciferin. It's part of the insects' mating ritual."

Despite his best efforts a small snort of laughter escaped him. He tried to hide it with a cough and throat clearing. "The hell you say?"

"Quite true. I recall Uncle Waldo explaining the phenomenon to me when I was very small. How should we count, do you think? Perhaps if we divided the area into quadrants and—"

Sawyer kissed her.

"—each of us—"

He kissed her again. "Open your mouth a little, sweetheart. Ah, that's it."

Her mouth was incredibly sweet.

Her tongue was incredibly sensuous.

Her moan nearly drove him wild.

A million fireflies lit up inside him.

She sighed when he pulled away. Why did she have to make those sexy little noises? It only made him want to go on kissing her.

And more.

He sucked in a deep, shuddering breath, tucked her head into the crook of his shoulder, and laid his cheek against the top of her head. Neither spoke. With one foot he pushed the swing and it lulled them gently.

After a few moments she asked drowsily, "Why didn't you go to school?"

"It's a long, boring story."

She wiggled closer and splayed her small hand over his chest. He could damned near feel the imprint of it sear through his shirt.

"I can't imagine anything about you being boring."

He hesitated. The first eighteen years of his life were part of his history that he preferred to forget and rarely discussed. But for some reason he wanted to share it with Pip. He wanted to share everything with her.

"I was born with a congenital heart defect." He felt her fingers tense against his chest, and he stroked the back of her hand. "It's okay now, but for a long time I was an invalid. The smallest exertion would tire me and send my mother into fits, so I spent most of my childhood in bed wishing I could climb trees and play baseball like a normal kid. Anyhow, I couldn't go to school, so I had tutors."

"As lively as you are, having to stay in bed must have been frustrating," Pip said.

"You can't imagine. And, as his only child, a big disappointment for my father. He played semipro ball for a while and was a big sports fan. So was my grandfather, Mirth Hayes. He's the one who started Mirth Bat Factory."

She lifted her head and looked at him. "That evolved into Mirth, Incorporated?"

He nodded.

"Did you outgrow the heart problem?"

"Nope. I had surgery the day after I turned eighteen. Dr. Denton Cooley fixed me up, right as rain. It was great. After a few months I could do anything I wanted to." He grinned. "Wanna see my scar?"

When she started unbuttoning the placket

of his polo shirt and pulling it down, he laughed and caught her hands. "I was only kidding. Anyway, it's too dark out here to see." She gently ran her fingertips down his sternum. Her touch made his throat ache and his repaired heart thump like crazy.

"I can feel it. Why did you wait so long to have surgery?"

He heaved a big sigh. "My mother. It was a risky procedure, and she would go into hysterics whenever the subject was mentioned. My father died in a car accident when I was eight, and she was even worse after that. I begged and begged, told her I was willing to take the risk, but she wouldn't hear of it. She told me that it was too expensive, that we couldn't afford it."

"I'm sure that she wanted only the best for you."

"No, my mother was a neurotic, self-obsessed woman. She still is. I didn't know it then, but my grandfather had offered to pay for the procedure. Mother refused to allow him to mention it to me. But when I was about ten or eleven, I got interested in the stock market, read everything I could find about it, and discovered I had a real knack for picking winners. And I started designing games. There wasn't much for me to do except read, watch TV, and entertain myself.

"Following the market, I parlayed my birthday and Christmas money into a nice sum and put it into a trust fund. As a teenager I also designed several games that are still the bread and butter of Mirth. Granddad manufactured them for me, and the royalties went into the fund as well.

"By the time I was fourteen, I'd accumulated more than enough to have the operation. But my mother had vapors every time I brought up the subject. Maybe if Granddad had lived, we could have talked her into it sooner, but he died a few weeks before my fifteenth birthday. As a minor I had no control over my money or my destiny."

"But when you were eighteen . . ."

"I took control of my life and checked into the hospital."

In a sweetly sensuous move Pip's lips softly touched the top of the scar, then she nestled her cheek against it. "And you lived happily ever after."

He kissed the top of her head. "I've tried."

She snuggled close to his warmth and said drowsily, "We have a lot in common. You had a lost childhood, too, didn't you?"

"Yep." *Two misfits*, he thought, not voicing the words.

"Where is your mother now?"

"Living in a very expensive condo in Florida and playing bridge with her cronies. She never really forgave me for defying her. We don't have much contact."

Her fingers stroked the length of his sternum. "She doesn't know what she's missing. You're very special."

"Thanks. *Merci*." With one foot he kept up the swing's gentle motion. After a few moments he heard her breathing change and felt her body relax.

For a long time Sawyer simply held the sleeping Pip. He counted fireflies. And he counted his blessings that the absolute perfect woman for him had come into his life.

"Heaven help me," he whispered into her hair. "I already love you."

FIVE

"Red alert! Red alert! Rise and shine!"

With the shouting and a raucous, clanging din, Pip came instantly awake and jackknifed up. Sawyer stood at the foot of her bed, grinning and banging on a pot with a large spoon. She scraped back her hair and squinted at him.

"What are you doing here?" she asked.

"I'm your morning wake-up call." He plopped down on a corner of the mattress. "You zonked out last night, so Nan and I put you to bed. Seemed silly to fly home for just a few hours, so I slept in the guest room."

"*You* and Nan put me to bed?"

"Truth is, I only carried you. She did most

of the putting. I offered to help, but that Nan's a hard-hearted woman. Told me to skedaddle." He pinched her toe and wiggled it. "It's time to rise and shine, Sleeping Beauty. Got a lot to do today, and we're burnin' daylight. Now, for breakfast do you want French toast, French Toast, or French toast?"

"French toast?"

He winked and flashed her a broad grin. "You're on. It's my specialty. By the time you're dressed, it'll be on the table."

"Where's Nan?"

"Gave her the day off. I believe she's going to visit her sister." He clapped his hands. "Let's hit the shower, troop."

"Troop?"

"Can't have troops with only one trooper. Come on, up you go."

Pip stayed exactly where she was and pulled the sheet closer to her chest. "I can't get up until you leave."

"Why not?"

"I'm not dressed."

His grin became more impish. "I noticed." He glanced at the mirror on the dresser.

Pip's gaze followed his. While she'd been careful to cover her front, both the back and side views of her skimpy nightgown were plainly visible in the mirror's reflection.

He reached over and ran his finger under the spaghetti strap at her shoulder. "I like your outfit. Very sexy."

His touch sent shivers over her sleep-warmed body. The intimacy of such a simple act surprised her. And made her leery. She wasn't accustomed to engaging in suggestive banter in her bedroom.

Gathering the sheet around her, she replied, "It's not sexy. It's cool and comfortable."

"Looks damned sexy to me." He moved closer and kissed her briefly. "Damned sexy."

"I think you'd better start breakfast."

Sawyer lifted her chin with one finger, and his expression sobered. "Pip, you aren't afraid of me, are you?"

"Of course not. Whatever gave you such a strange idea?"

"Maybe it's because you're as jumpy as a grasshopper on a hot griddle." His knuckle lightly grazed the curve of her chin. "You don't have to be afraid of me. I'd never push you farther than you want to go. If I ever make you uncomfortable, just tell me to back off, and I will. Okay?" He smiled.

"Okay. Back off. I need to dress. In private."

"Well, damn." He slapped his leg, grinned, and stood. "I think there's an old saying about being hoisted by my own petard that fits here. I never did know what a petard was."

She laughed. "A petard was an explosive device used in medieval times for blowing open barricades and fortifications. Since the gunpowder devices were rather crude in those days, often the person who set the charge was blown up with the barricade. I think Shakespeare is credited with popularizing the expression."

"How about that." Amusement stole through him. "I think I'm going to go home and throw away my encyclopedia."

"Why would you do that?"

With his fists bearing his weight against the mattress on either side of her, he bent down and dropped a quick kiss on her nose. "Because I've found a better one with fantastic legs. Do you like light cinnamon or heavy?"

She frowned, pondering the sense of his question.

"On your French toast."

"Light."

"You're on. And"—he winked—"wear shorts today." Whistling, he left the room.

❖━━━━━━━━❖

"You game?" Sawyer couldn't keep the laughter from his voice as he looked from Pip to Astroworld's famous roller coaster, the Texas Cyclone.

Her beautiful pansy-purple eyes were as big as Orphan Annie's. But not as blank. Though she tried to hide it, her apprehension grew as the line in front of them shortened.

"You've given everything a go from having your caricature drawn to trying the Batman ride. This is the *pièce de résistance*." He shot her a lopsided grin. "That's French, you know, for—"

"I know what it's French for," she said huffily. She eyed the huge wooden construction. "Are you sure it's safe?"

"Positive. I wouldn't let Scooter, Davy, and the other kids ride it if it weren't safe."

"Those children ride this thing?"

"Yep. Make a beeline for it as soon as we're through the gate."

"Have you ridden it before?"

"Dozens of times."

She took a deep breath. "I'm game. I only wish I hadn't eaten that last hot dog."

He laughed and slipped his fingers through hers when the attendant motioned them forward. She damned near cut off the circulation in his hand, but wisely he kept his mouth shut.

One of the things that had become evident during their day at the theme park was that Pip was courageous. And a good sport. She'd tried everything that he'd suggested. And had a ball. She'd laughed in the fun house and driven bumper cars with a vengeance.

His only criticism—and he'd never in a million years voice it—was that she was so damned intense. He had a hunch that it would take a while for her to learn to relax and enjoy the fun times instead of going at them as if she were fighting fire.

When their turn came, she marched to her place with all the enthusiasm of royalty headed to the guillotine. And with as much dignity. After they were secured in their seat, he said, "Last chance to change your mind."

Her chin went up. "I'm not changing my mind."

With a rumble and a roar they were off.

At the first big drop her eyes widened, then squinched shut. She didn't utter a peep, but she buried her head against his chest and grabbed a wad of his shirt front. As they climbed, dropped, looped, and zipped high over the park, she clung to him, her knuckles whiter, her head burrowed deeper. He held her tightly, but his words of comfort were blown away by the wind and lost in the screams of the riders.

When their car coasted to a stop, Pip looked decidedly green. Alarmed, he brushed the wisps of hair from her damp forehead. "Are you okay?"

She shook her head. "That hot dog is rebelling. I have to get to a bathroom."

He quickly led her to the ladies' room and would have gone inside with her if a couple of women hadn't complained loudly when he tried.

While he waited, he crammed his hands in his pockets and shifted from one foot to the other, cursing himself for every kind of fool he could think of. Hadn't he noticed her nervousness? Why had he been so blasted intent on getting her on that roller coaster?

He wanted to beat his head against the wall.

Hell, it would serve him right if she told him to buzz off like the idiot he was.

After what seemed like hours she emerged,

pale and shaky, with eyes downcast and an embarrassed smile on her lovely lips. For the first time since he'd awakened from his heart surgery, he wanted to cry.

Hands on her shoulders, he searched her face. "Sweetheart, I'm so sorry. So damned sorry. I deserve a swift kick in the butt. Here, kick me." He turned and bent over. "Kick me. Hard."

"Sawyer," she hissed. "I'm not going to kick you."

"I want you to. I deserve it. Hard. Right here." He slapped his bottom.

"Sawyer! Get up. People are staring."

Hell, he didn't care. He addressed the small crowd that gathered. "I've been a complete idiot. Somebody ought to kick me. You want to? Or you?"

A teenage boy in high-tops and a creative haircut ambled over. He shrugged. "If it floats your boat, I'll give it a shot."

"You will not," Pip stated firmly. She grabbed Sawyer's arm and dragged him away. "Nan would say that you're crazier than a bessie bug."

He noticed that she was smiling. "Does this mean I'm forgiven?"

"You've nothing to be forgiven for. It was

my choice and my stomach. But I would like to have a Coke before I try it again."

His brows lifted. "You want to ride it again?"

"Certainly. I'm no quitter." She hooked her arm through his. "Until I became queasy, I loved it."

Sawyer's chest swelled. "Damn, you're some kind of woman."

"Exactly what kind is that?"

Tenderness filled him to overflowing. "My kind."

Late in the afternoon, exhausted to her toes and feeling wilted from the warm day, Pip sat sprawled in a padded patio chair on Sawyer's third-floor deck that sat nestled amid the treetops. She held her face to the cool breeze that swayed the uppermost branches and rustled through the new leaves.

Sawyer leaned against the wooden railing of the large red-cedar expanse, grinning at her as usual and looking as fresh as when they'd begun that morning.

"Tired?" he asked.

"Totally and completely pooped. Where do you get all your energy?"

"I saved it up for eighteen years. Want something to drink?"

"About a gallon of something very cold and very wet."

"Cocktail? Beer? Cola? Lemonade? Water?"

"Lemonade sounds perfect."

"Lemonade it is. If Mrs. Tinker, my handy-dandy housekeeper, has lemons in the fridge. Got a second choice?"

She fluttered her hand. "Whatever."

He dragged a footstool over to her, lifted her legs, and deposited them on the cushion. "Rest your tootsies while I rustle up the drinks." With his hands on the arms of her chair he leaned over and rubbed his nose against hers. "The day is young yet, and we still have dancing lessons to begin. What do you want to learn first? Fox-trot, swing? Maybe rumba?" His perfect teeth flashed as he took a few hip-swinging steps with an imaginary partner. "I'd love to see you rumba."

Rolling her eyes, Pip groaned. "I'm in no shape to dance."

Sawyer wiggled his brows. "*Au contraire*, m'dear. Your shape is perfect."

She laughed. "Go fix the drinks."

He made a sweeping bow. "Your wish is

my command. Just don't start the sunset without me."

"I'll speak to Mother Nature personally."

When he left, Pip toed off her sneakers and flexed her feet, then closed her eyes and soaked up the peacefulness of her surroundings. Though she wasn't exactly sure where it was located—in the helicopter she'd had no sense of direction—she loved Sawyer's home and its grounds. What she'd seen of them. All cedar and glass, the large house blended perfectly with the wooded area and the small creek that meandered through the property.

His house had surprised her. She'd figured him for an apartment located in the hub of Houston activity. But this was a retreat, a tree house in the forest. Nice. Very nice. Relaxing.

A weight landed in her lap. Startled, her eyes popped open. A large black cat sat studying her with squinted golden eyes.

Pip smiled. "Hello, kitty. Where did you come from?"

The cat only swished its tail and rubbed its head under her arm. When she started to stroke its fur, the cat settled in her lap, purring.

"I see you've met Shadow," Sawyer said, returning with a tray of drinks. "You should be honored. He's very selective about who he allows to pet him."

"I like animals, but I've never had a pet."

"Not even as a kid?"

She shook her head and stroked the length of Shadow's back. "My uncles are allergic to animal dander."

Sawyer set the tray on a table and handed Pip a frosty glass. "We were in luck. Mrs. Tinker had a pitcher of lemonade in the refrigerator. Sometimes I think that woman is psychic."

Pip took a long swallow. "Perfect. I don't know if she's psychic, but she makes delicious lemonade."

He dragged a chair close to hers, plopped down on it, kicked off his shoes, and propped up his feet next to hers on the stool. After taking a big swig from his drink, he rested the glass on his stomach and wiggled his toes. "Ahhh, this is the life."

"It's lovely here. I feel as if I'm in a big tree house."

"That's the idea. I always wanted one as a kid, didn't you?"

"I never really considered it."

He grinned. "Too busy with calculus and such?"

"I suppose so." She smiled as Shadow rubbed his head under her chin, then hopped down and sauntered away. "I want to thank you for the day. It was fun, wasn't it?"

"For sure. And the day is far from over. When you get your second wind, we have a date with a CD player. You like chicken casserole?"

"I'm not a finicky eater. Why?"

"Mrs. Tinker left a casserole and some other stuff for dinner. With the directions. I put the casserole in the oven. And don't worry about Nan. I told her that we'd probably be out late."

"You seem to think of everything."

"Yep. Look at that. Have you ever seen a more beautiful sunset?"

Truly she hadn't. As a variety of birds chirped a soft evening song, the leaves seemed to drip with gold. Through a break in the trees she had a clear view of the pink-and-purple-washed horizon with the huge orange sun hanging low in the sky and partially obscured by a gentle knoll thick with wildflowers. The beauty of the moment made her throat ache and a sheen of tears form in her eyes.

Pointing toward the knoll, she said, "Something about that area seems to have a magical quality. If I believed in such things, I would expect fairies to dance there."

Sawyer sucked in an exaggerated gasp. "You don't believe in fairies?"

"Certainly not." She chuckled. "And neither do you."

"But I do."

She rolled her eyes and glanced toward him. "You're such a tease that half the time people don't know when you're serious."

"I am serious. I believe in fairies. Didn't you hear Scooter say that the tooth fairy left a quarter under his pillow?" He winked, and she laughed.

"I didn't mean *that* kind of fairy. I meant the kind that lives in flowers and under toadstools."

"You mean you've never seen them?"

"Of course not. Such blarney is totally at variance with reality. There is absolutely no scientific proof for that sort of nonsense. And don't try to tell me that you've seen a fairy."

A smug smile on his face, he settled back against the chair cushion. "Okay, I won't tell you."

She gave him an exasperated look. He only smiled innocently as the silence stretched on interminably. Slowly his smile faded into a pensive expression, one faintly tinged with sadness. He reached for her hand and stroked the back of it with his thumb.

"What are you thinking?" she asked.

"Just wondering what it would be like to grow up without believing in fairies. I guess you didn't believe in Santa Claus as a kid either."

"My uncles thought that it was an insult to my intelligence to perpetrate myths such as Santa Claus. We had Christmas festivities, of course, but my gifts were from people, not an imaginary elf in a red suit."

Sawyer shifted in his chair. "My mother was lacking as a parent in lots of ways, but she was big on Santa Claus. Part of being a kid is enjoying fantasy and imagination. I remember lying in my bed and imagining that I could fly. Lord, I wanted to fly so badly I could taste it. I felt that if I believed enough, I could soar like Superman. Didn't you ever feel that?"

An old memory flitted through her head. "Once."

"And?" He leaned closer.

Remembering, she chuckled. "I must have been about six or seven. I'm not sure why

I decided to try it, but I got a tablecloth, fashioned it into crude wings attached to my arms with pins and rubber bands, and tried to fly from the hood of Uncle Emory's car."

"What happened?"

"Uncle Waldo stopped me before I broke anything. He explained that humans were physiologically unsuited to flight and went into some detail, with books and drawings, about the concepts of aerodynamics."

"How sad."

"It wasn't sad. It was very sensible. I never tried it again, and consequently I never broke my neck trying to do something impossible."

"Flying's not impossible," he said. "I do it all the time."

"In a *helicopter*, which is quite different."

"Not really. It's just an extension of my fantasy. Part of the magic of life." He rubbed her instep with the bottom of his socked foot.

"You know very well that being able to fly a helicopter has nothing to do with magic. It involves physics and aeronautical engineering."

"You explain it your way; I'll explain it mine. I prefer to believe in magic."

"You're incorrigible."

"Because I believe in magic? If there's no magic, how do you explain laughter, joy, and . . . love?"

"As I recall, it's a matter of behavioral conditioning and body chemistry."

"Ah, my sweet, I see that I have to do some serious deprogramming work with you." He stood and held out his hand. "Let's eat."

Standing by the deck's rail, they savored one last moment of sunset before they went inside.

They had dinner in a glassed-in nook off the kitchen. While they ate, they spotted a family of deer slipping through the woods and standing beside the stream. The two of them shared the scene in silence, watching as the animals moved gracefully through the gathering dusk and bent to drink.

Touched by the simple beauty of the animals, Pip pondered the notion that, truly, something about the place, the moment, almost did seem enchanted. As if a spell had been cast about them.

Not that she admitted it to Sawyer. He'd be off on another of his tales about fairies and magic. She realized that he was teasing her, but . . . sometimes she wondered. He wasn't like anyone she'd ever encountered. He was different. No. He was *unique*. But in a very pleasant sense of the word.

She popped the last bite of roll into her mouth and glanced up. He was gazing at her intently.

"What are you thinking about?" she asked.

He reached to where her arm rested on the table and slowly ran his index finger along its length from elbow to fingertips, leaving a trail of tactile awareness. His thumb stroked the inside of her ring finger, raising chill bumps on her skin and sending tingles straight to her belly.

"About magic. About you. About how absolutely adorable you are. About how crazy I am over you. About how badly I want to kiss you and hold you and touch you."

The bite of roll lodged in her throat. She had to swallow three times to move it past the constriction. Her heart surged; a sudden warmth rushed over her; her pulse went wildly erratic.

She wanted the same thing.

But she was nervous. Excruciatingly nervous.

"We need to clear the table," she said, jumping up and fumbling with plates and silverware.

"Chick-en."

Ignoring his comment—which was maddeningly on target—she stacked the dishes and carried them to the counter.

He took the things from her hands, set them down, and turned her toward them. "Leave them. Mrs. Tinker takes care of the dishes." He lifted her chin until their eyes met. "You can't ignore it; you can't escape it. I'm falling in love with you. And I want you. It's magic. And perfectly natural."

She tried to speak, but her voice failed. All she could do was feel. And the feelings were so strange, so potent, that they puzzled her. Made her anxious.

His mouth moved slowly toward hers. "I'm going to kiss you. Okay?"

She lifted her face to him and nodded as his lips met hers. The tip of his tongue teased the seam of her lips until they parted and allowed him to enter and explore.

The kiss, at first incredibly sweet, began to change into a more demanding contact. His hands slid over her back, then lower to cup her bottom and draw her closer.

An unaccustomed wildness streaked through her, and she wrapped her arms tightly around him, wanting to blend her body into his. Her tongue darted into his mouth in imitation of his, and he groaned.

He broke contact with her lips and hugged her close, his temple against hers. His breathing ragged beside her ear, he moaned, "Oh, love, you set me on fire."

Stroking the curve of her hips, he nuzzled her cheek and pressed his lips along the underside of her jaw. She lifted her chin to encourage access to the sensitive area. He obliged by tracing moist, deliciously erotic circles with his tongue, and she became lost in sensation.

An irritating noise penetrated her awareness. First dimly, then stridently. Sawyer muttered something slightly profane about beepers, let her go, and checked the device on his belt.

"It's Mirth Ranch," he said. "I'll give them a quick call." He touched the tip of her nose. "You stay right here and hold my place."

He dialed from the kitchen phone and, after a brief exchange, frowned and hung up.

"Something wrong?"

"Scooter's feverish, and now Davy is getting sick. It's probably nothing major, but I'd better check on them. It shouldn't take too long. We can still—"

Pip shook her head. "I'm tired. Why don't we save the dancing lessons for another time?"

He grinned. "I'd forgotten all about the dancing lessons."

Pip was reading in bed when the phone rang a few hours later.

"Davy is fine. He was having sympathy symptoms, but Scooter has German measles," Sawyer said. "He was supposed to be innoculated against them, but either somebody slipped up or his shot didn't take. You ever had them?"

"Probably. I don't recall. But I vividly remember having chicken pox. They were awful."

They talked for half an hour and ended with Sawyer's promise to be over bright and early the next morning. "You like to roller-skate?" he asked.

"I don't know. I've never tried it."

"*Never?*"

"Nope. But I can ride a bike."

"Great. I'll bring my bike with me."

After she hung up, Pip turned out the light and snuggled under the cover. Sleep eluded her. Sawyer's face invaded her mind, and his laughter echoed in her ears. She touched her lips, savoring the memory of his mouth on hers. At the recollection her body quickened.

Sawyer Hayes had stirred a feminine part of her that she hadn't known existed. Now it had awakened with a vengeance. She was eager to explore this new phenomenon.

She stretched and became instantly aware of the sensuous feel of her silk gown and the cotton sheets against her skin. She'd never noticed how profoundly texture could act as a tactile stimulator. Nor had she ever considered herself a hedonist, but with the thought of Sawyer's hands on her skin, her body's external sensory receptors seemed to heighten tenfold, and an unfamiliar longing pulsed inside.

She stretched again and squirmed slightly, enjoying the heady sensation of fabric against skin and a sweet throb low in her body.

Exactly how, she wondered, did this fit in with her program for *Accelerated Remediation of Social Development*?

She'd read up on the developmental aspects tomorrow. Tonight . . . tonight she'd simply luxuriate in the experience.

SIX

His eyebrows drawn into a bushy black line, Leonard Hooker stormed into Sawyer's office. "Where in the hell have you been for the past two weeks, boy?"

Sawyer looked up from his task—lacing a new pair of skates custom-made for Pip. "Hello, Uncle Len. I've been . . . around."

"Around? Around where? You damned sure haven't been around this office. How do you expect to run a business if you never show up?"

Sawyer put aside the skates, reared back in his chair, and propped his feet up on his desk. "The same way I've run it for years: Pay you a damned good salary along with a quarter interest in the company to handle operations. You tired of the job, Uncle Len? If you are, Herb Burkhalter could probably take over for you."

Hooker back-peddled in a hurry. "No, no. I've just been concerned about you. I never know what hare—er—project you're involved in. Like to be kept informed."

"I've been spending a lot of time with Pip— Dr. LeBaron." And he had.

They'd been to dinner and to movies; they'd been on long bike rides. They'd gone to a baseball game at the Dome and fed the seals at the zoo. He'd been teaching her to skate and to dance. And besides charming the boys at the ranch every time they visited, she was getting to be pretty good on Blossom. Sometimes they'd spent entire afternoons watching clouds, finding figures in the sky, and talking. And laughing.

She'd even managed to teach him a little French, but he'd had a hard time concentrating. He'd never realized before what a kissable language French was. Most of the words puckered her lips in such an enticing way that he couldn't think about learning, only about kissing her.

A lascivious gleam came into Hooker's eyes as he sank into the chair in front of Sawyer's desk. "Ah, Dr. LeBaron, the person we need on the virtual reality project. Making any headway with her?"

"Headway?" He'd spent a good bit of time kissing her, holding her, touching her. But wanting more. A lot more. Still, he'd kept his promise to himself and was taking it slow and easy.

"Has she agreed to come aboard?"

"Uh, not exactly."

"Not *exactly*. What does that mean?"

"She's fully committed to another project at the moment." Sawyer tried his damnedest to keep a straight face. His uncle would blow a gasket if he knew the details.

Sawyer had learned over the years how to handle his overbearing uncle, who'd been a career navy man until he'd resigned his commission to help Sawyer get Mirth, Inc. going. Usually he simply listened while Uncle Len lectured, then did as he pleased.

His and Leonard Hooker's management philosophies were poles apart. His uncle preferred an autocratic style while Sawyer's—if it could be called a style—was definitely laid-back. Ordinarily Sawyer was content to focus on research and development and let his uncle run things, stepping in only to keep a governor on Len's domineering ways or smooth the feathers that he ruffled.

There had been times in the past couple of years that Sawyer had considered asking his uncle, who was his mother's older brother, to retire, but Len didn't seem ready, and Sawyer didn't have the heart to fire him. He remembered that his uncle had sacrificed his naval career to help his sister and nephew run the business after Granddad Hayes died and they'd discovered that the man who'd taken over the management of the bat factory had been lining his own pockets with the company profits. In truth Len was a good businessman. Sawyer was an idea person; he hated the boring detail of day-to-day management operations. He and his uncle, with their differing methods and talents, made a good team. But mostly he couldn't forget that the same people who wouldn't give a kid who was trying to start a corporation the time of day had rolled out the red carpet for the mature, confident, and commanding retired naval captain. He owed Leonard. And Sawyer was loyal.

"Have you tried upping the ante?" Hooker asked.

Sawyer frowned. He'd lost the thread of their conversation. "For what?"

"For *what*? Hell, boy, haven't you been listening? Have you tried offering Dr. LeBaron more money? If we don't snap her up quick, somebody else will. This virtual reality business is hot right now, and experts in the field are hard to come by. Get your head out of the sand and sign her to a contract. If you can't, I damned well can."

Fury flashed through Sawyer. His feet hit the floor. He slapped his palms on his desk and leaned over, glaring at his uncle. "You stay the hell away from Pip, do you hear me? And I'm going to remind you one more time that *I'm* the president and chairman of the board of Mirth. I'll do what I please, when I please. Is that clear?"

Hooker's mouth thinned and his nostrils flared, but he kept silent.

Finally his uncle stood, his bearing as stiff as that of an academy cadet. "Perfectly." He wheeled and left.

"Oh, hell," Sawyer muttered, swiping his hand across his face.

He hated these confrontations. And they seemed to be coming more frequently. Reluctant as he was to admit it, the time was nearing when he'd have to ask for his uncle's resignation. He'd hired Herb Burkhalter a couple of years earlier to groom him for the vice-president/CEO position. And Herb was good. A good business mind, good with people. Not abrasive like Len.

He buzzed his secretary. "Gloria, did you get those concert tickets?"

"Sure did, boss. Had to pay a scalper a pretty penny, but you now have the best seats in the house," she replied. "But tell me, exactly who or what is Wretched Xcess?"

Inside the Summit, lights flashed in a dizzying display, amps thundered and shrieked, and the crowd went wild as the hard-rock band performed their latest hit on the stage. Sawyer got more of a kick out of watching Pip, her eyes wide and mouth agape.

"How do you like it?" he yelled over the screaming crowd and ear-shattering music.

"What?" she shouted back.

He leaned close to her ear and yelled his question again.

"It's . . . interesting."

He laughed and joined in the rhythmic clapping, elbowing Pip until she joined in as well. She wasn't exactly on beat, but she was trying.

Eventually people started jostling them, shoving forward or standing on their seats. The crowd became so boisterous that Sawyer got nervous.

"Are you ready to leave?" he shouted.

"Only if you are."

"Let's get out of here."

Outside, as they walked down the ramp, Pip splayed her hand across her chest and breathed deeply. "I think I'm having culture shock. My heart is racing, and my entire body is quaking. Is that normal?"

Laughing, Sawyer hooked his arm around her waist, drew her close, and kissed her forehead. "Perfectly normal." Her arm went around his waist, and his hand slipped lower to ride the crest of her hip. "The music really revs you up, doesn't it?"

Did that explain, she wondered, why at that moment she had a powerful urge to grab him by the hair, kiss him savagely, and roll around on the grass with him? She was much too civilized to do such a scandalous thing, of course, but the feelings were definitely there. She shivered.

"Something wrong?" he asked.

"No. Not a thing."

Liar, she chided herself. The music,

designed to stimulate sexual excitement, had accomplished its mission. More and more she was realizing how very ready she was for their relationship to escalate into something beyond steamy kisses and sensuous caresses. Hadn't she gritted her teeth, broken out in a sweat, and practically panted while she'd stayed up half the night reading *Joy of Sex*?

Such overwhelming emotions were alien to her. She had tried to apply reason and logic to the situation, but her feelings had nothing to do with logic. Her desire quotient far exceeded her intelligence quotient.

The simple fact was: She wanted him.

For the first time in her life Marguerite Elizabeth LeBaron, Ph.D., had the hots for a man.

But she wasn't confident enough to tell him so. What if he didn't want her? Lord, she would die of mortification if he teased her about her feelings. Was she normal?

She would call Carol Venhuizen. After all, Carol was a psychologist. She would know.

Pip shoved the remains of their picnic lunch into a plastic bag and stowed it in the hamper.

She cast lingering glances toward Sawyer, who lay stretched out, stomach down, on a blanket spread among the wildflowers on the knoll near his house.

Her reaction to him *was* perfectly normal, thank heavens. Carol had said so . . . after she'd stopped laughing. Pip hadn't considered her questions amusing. But the tall blonde with keen blue eyes said the same thing Sawyer said frequently: "Lighten up. Enjoy yourself." She'd also added, "Sounds like you're experiencing a delayed puberty. Experiment a little . . . but keep your head."

While she was willing to experiment a little, Pip wondered if she could keep her head. Things were moving so quickly that she didn't have much control of her head lately. Sawyer seemed to fill it entirely. When they were apart, he constantly invaded her thoughts. Her dreams.

And when they were together—which was most of her waking hours—she couldn't focus on anything but him. It was disconcerting. Like now. She couldn't keep her eyes off him.

Elbows resting on the edge of the spread, he was searching through a patch of clover. His position bunched the muscles of his back and shoulders, and she longed to slide her hand over the hardness that fascinated her so and feel the corded ridges so different from her own body.

But she didn't.

She admired the tautness of his buttocks, the way his thighs strained the fabric of his jeans. And his hair. The sun brought out the red glints of his thick, unruly thatch with its charming cowlicks. Her fingers itched to thread themselves through the errant strands and test their texture.

But she didn't.

She set the hamper aside and stretched out near him. "What are you searching for so diligently?"

"A four-leaf clover."

"Why?"

"Because if I find one, I'll have good luck."

She snorted. "You don't seriously believe in luck, do you?"

"Sure I do. How do you think I got this far in life?"

"By hard work and ingenuity, I imagine."

"Nope. Pure luck. I have a whole book of pressed four-leaf clovers that I started collecting as a kid. Some of the only times I was allowed out of bed was to lie on a quilt in the backyard on mild days. I remember how excited I was when I found the first four-leafer. That's about the time I started playing the stock market with my Christmas and birthday money. And winning. It was pure luck."

"Pure coincidence. Four-leaf clovers are simply botanical mutants, nothing more."

"Maybe so, but just in case, why don't you help me look? And to make it interesting, we'll have a contest. The one who finds the most in an hour will win a prize."

"What sort of prize?" she asked.

"Loser buys dinner tomorrow night at Vargo's."

Her eyes narrowed. Pip loved a challenge. "You're on."

Once she agreed, Pip devoted the same degree of concentration to searching the clumps of clover that she did to every project she undertook. Rather than use the haphazard ripple and scan method that Sawyer preferred, she used twigs to divide each stand into a grid so that she could examine it systematically.

Soon lost in her quest, she was surprised when Sawyer called, "Time!"

"An hour can't be up."

He grinned. "Actually it was two. But you look so cute when you're engrossed that I didn't have the heart to stop you. How many did you find?"

She held out the napkin that she'd used to lay them on. "Five. How many did you find?"

"Five." He held up his small bundle by the stems. "Looks like we have a tie. Should we make dinner Dutch?" He grinned impishly. "Or do you want a sudden-death pick-off?"

" 'Sudden death'? That sounds ominous."

"Nope. The first person to find one wins."

"Agreed."

Sawyer spotted one right away, but he didn't pick it. Instead he kept his gaze on Pip. Down on her knees and elbows, her cute little tush molded by denim shorts and poking up in the air, she was jabbing sticks in the ground.

Watching her made him smile inside and out. And it strained the buttons on his jeans considerably.

God, he was nuts about her.

No, he was wildly, madly in love with her. He thought it was love. It must be love, he reasoned, or why else would he be filled with such a sweet ache? There was a powerful sexual attraction there, all right—he stayed aroused and walked funny half of the time—but he felt more than a physical need.

He wanted to tuck her under his arm and leap tall buildings in a single bound, fly to distant planets and play tag among the stars, wrap the world in silver paper and lay it under her Christmas tree.

"I found one!" she shouted.

The force of her smile smacked him right in the solar plexus and almost brought him to his knees. "The hell you say!"

She giggled. "Looks like dinner is on you." She brushed her knees and sank down to the blanket, her arms propping her from behind, her face lifted to the late sun.

He joined her.

Reaching for her thick braid, he drew it over her shoulder and carefully tucked each of his four-leaf clovers among the plaited strands.

"Aren't you going to press them?" she asked.

He shook his head. "Finding you was the luckiest thing that ever happened to me."

Using the curly dark tuft at the end of her braid, he slowly traced the scooped neck of her red tank top, his eyes greedily following the path.

Pip sucked in a breath, and he smiled. As her hair and his gaze swept over the swell of her breasts, chill bumps rushed over her skin, and her nipples hardened. She wanted to say something, to do something. Instead she remained very still.

His fingers replaced the tuft and traveled in a leisurely fashion back and forth, back and forth over her sun-warmed skin. She sucked in a deeper breath, and the back of his fingers slipped below the neckline to continue the stroking.

When his nail tips moved across her nipples, her diaphragm convulsed and her head dropped back.

"Feel good?" he asked softly.

"It feels . . . it feels . . . wonderful."

"Feels wonderful to me too. This will feel even better."

He replaced his fingers with his tongue and drew the straps of her tank top down. Lower and lower and lower until her nipples were bared to the spring air, the warm sun, and his tongue. He circled each tip, and the breeze conspired with the wetness he left to turn her breasts to a sweet agony of sensation.

When his mouth closed around one nipple and gently sucked, she gasped with surprise, then strained toward the source of such delicious pleasure.

Lying on her back and experiencing only his

lips, teeth, and tongue on her breasts, she was soon reduced to a writhing mass of nerve endings with no thoughts, only feelings. Mind-boggling feelings. Delightful feelings. Erotic feelings.

Threading her fingers through his hair, she pulled against his head, arched toward him, trying to draw him closer. Closer.

His mouth and his tongue went wild as if filled with a devouring hunger to consume her completely. Guttural sounds from his throat blended with similar sounds from hers. She felt magnificently pagan. Earthy. Primitive.

Wet kisses covered her breasts, then his mouth moved lower as he bared her midriff and fumbled with the button at the waistband of her shorts. The zipper slid open under the onslaught of his questing hand. His fingers slipped beneath the scanty fabric of her panties, then stopped abruptly.

"Love," he whispered, "are you protected?"

Blinking rapidly, she fought through a sensual haze. "Protected?"

"You know. *Protected*."

"Ohhh. Birth control. No."

He uttered a succinct profanity, sat up, propped his elbows on his knees, his forehead in his hands, and took several deep, ragged breaths. "I don't have anything either."

"What about at your house?"

"Honey, if I did, I'd set a new world's record for the hundred-yard dash." She giggled. He laughed. "Aren't we a fine pair?"

"Sawyer, I'm sorry. I didn't think. I mean, it never occurred to me. Well, I simply didn't consider—"

He leaned over, kissed her gently, and pulled her tank top back into place. He kissed her tummy as gently before he restored her zipper and button. "*I* did. I haven't thought about much else since I first met you, but I hadn't planned for things to get out of hand."

"Were they out of hand? I was rather enjoying myself."

He tugged on her braid. "Me, too, love. Me, too." His brows drew together, and he regarded her seriously for a moment. "How old are you? Twenty-six? It's not possible that—naw."

"What's not possible?"

Lifting her chin, he looked deeply into her eyes. "Have you ever made love before?"

She swallowed and stuck her nose in the air. "I don't think that my past experience is any of your concern."

He smiled at her tenderly. "It is if you're a virgin."

He waited for her reply. None came. When the silence became interminable, he asked again, "Are you?"

She looked away. "Am I what?"

"Dammit, you are." He spat out a few colorful curses.

Her hackles went up. "It's not as if I have the plague, you know."

He stood and drew her into his arms. "I know. I'm not angry with you. I'm angry with myself. A woman's first time should be special, romantic. I was going after you like a boar in heat."

Her heart almost stopped. A huge lump formed in her throat. She didn't want to ask, but she had to. "Does this mean that you don't intend to make love to me?"

He grinned a slow, lascivious grin. "Oh, I intend to make love to you, all right. But I also intend for it to be special. Give me a couple of days to work on it."

They gathered their things and went back to Sawyer's house.

In the second-floor game room, which was filled with a fifties-style jukebox and Sawyer's collection of vintage pinball machines, they tried to play a few games, but they scored badly. They were both too aware of the new turn their relationship had taken to concentrate on pinball.

They put together dinner from odds and ends in the refrigerator, but neither of them ate much. Shadow twined around their legs soliciting choice morsels from their plates until, sated, he licked his whiskers and wandered off.

The phone rang.

Sawyer ignored it, but the ringing persisted.

"Hadn't you better get that?"

He shook his head. "The answering machine will pick it up. If it were an emergency, important people have my beeper number. It's probably my mother again."

"Don't you want to talk to her?"

"Not particularly. I talked to her yesterday. All she did was bitch. I think Uncle Len sicced her on to me."

Pip frowned. "About what?"

"My uncle and I have different views on my participation in the company, my work habits, Mirth Ranch, profit margins, and almost everything. He's been trying to 'talk some sense into me.' When I don't follow his advice, he enlists my mother's aid in harping on me."

"I don't understand. I thought you were the president of the company."

"I am. But Uncle Len is a regimented kind of guy—his military background, I guess. I'm not. Eight-to-five, forty-hour weeks don't suit me. His work ethic and mine don't match. It bugs the hell out of him."

Pip toyed with a potato chip on her plate. She'd been so preoccupied with having fun with Sawyer in the past few weeks that she hadn't considered his position. "You *have* been spending a great deal of time with me. Have I taken you away from your work? Have you even been to your office since we met?"

"A couple of times. And I've loved spending time with you. I have all the money I'll ever need; my mother is financially secure. The company's going strong. I work when I feel like it." He grinned. "I prefer to play."

She hesitated to say so, but his attitude did seem rather . . . immature. And at complete variance with her own. For most of her life work had been her primary focus. One's work *was* one's life.

Deciding to venture into a safer area, she asked, "Why is your uncle opposed to Mirth Ranch? It's such a fine endeavor. You've given those boys a chance. And they love you for it."

"Bottom line? Profit margin. Operating the ranch costs a bundle. If he were totally in charge, closing it down would be his number-one priority."

Pip was aghast. "Surely not."

"Yep. He's told me so a dozen times. It's a major bone of contention between us. And one of the reasons I'd never step aside for him."

Back in the game room they danced for a while to golden-oldies ballads played on the jukebox—rather they held each other and swayed in time to music. It was sweet torment.

Finally they gave up all pretense of dancing and simply held each other. Even in her skimpy attire the room seemed stifling to Pip. Either she had a fever or his nearness was short-circuiting her internal thermostat. Feeling agitated and overwhelmed with longing, her entire body trembled against his. She felt his tremble as well.

"Are you thinking about what I'm thinking about?" Sawyer asked.

"I don't know," she replied. "I was wondering if we could find a drugstore open."

He burst into laughter and hugged her tight. "Not tonight, love. I promised you something special, and that's one promise I'm going to keep."

Two nights later Pip lay in bed, restless. She'd spent all day with Sissy Strahan at a Girl Scout function that had been planned for a long time. She hadn't seen Sawyer since the night before.

And she missed him. Terribly.

She hadn't realized how totally he'd insinuated himself into her life until she hadn't seen him for twenty-four hours.

She punched her pillow and rearranged her position. Sleep eluded her. Turning over, she was about to punch her pillow again when she heard a faint noise against her windowpane. Keeping very still, she listened.

Another small *crack*. Then another. And another.

Tossing back the covers but leaving the lights off, she sneaked to the window of her second-floor bedroom and peered around the curtain. By the dim grounds lighting she could make out a male figure, sitting on a tree limb not three feet from her window.

It didn't occur to her to be frightened. She recognized the shape of a familiar green baseball cap. Raising the window, she leaned on the sill and stuck her head out.

"Sawyer," she whispered loudly, "what are you doing in the tree?"

He scooted toward her, flashing a bright smile. "I missed you."

"What were you throwing at my window?"

"M&M's." He stuck out a big bag. "With almonds. Want some?"

"No, thanks."

"Get some clothes on and come with me. I have a surprise for you."

"What is it?"

"If I told you, Short Stuff, it wouldn't be a surprise. You'll like it. Come on."

"But it's late, and Nan is asleep."

"So? Don't you ever sneak out of the house at night?"

"Certainly not. I've never had a reason."

"You have one now. Leave Nan a note if you think she'll worry. But we'll be back before she misses you. Come on."

Grabbing shorts, top, and sneakers, Pip hurried to the bathroom to dress. When she came out, Sawyer was sitting astride the windowsill waiting.

He waved her toward him. "Come on. This way."

"Why don't we go out the front door?"

"Naw, this way's more fun. Haven't you ever climbed a tree?"

She rolled her eyes.

"No, guess not," he said. "It's time you learned."

With Sawyer giving instructions every step of the way, she finally made it down the big oak.

A few minutes later they were in his sports car headed toward Houston. "Where are we going?" she asked.

"Main Street. Downtown."

"But, Sawyer, it's almost midnight. Everything will be closed."

He grinned. "I know. It's perfect."

SEVEN

Pip sat on the bus-stop bench while Sawyer finished tying the laces on her Rollerblades. She adjusted her kneepads, stood, and peeked out one side of the shelter. The broad downtown thoroughfare was completely deserted with only an occasional taxi passing on the streets.

Nervously she glanced at Sawyer. "Are you sure this is legal?"

He grinned. "I've never had a problem."

"You've done this before?"

As he buckled his helmet, his grin widened. "Sure."

"Why don't I believe you?"

Laughing, he took her hand, and they started to glide down the wide sidewalk alongside one of the major department stores.

Being in the heart of the deserted city, with tall buildings looming all around and street-lights casting their eerie glow, felt a bit bizarre. And sort of exciting. At least she assumed that excitement pumped the adrenaline rush she experienced.

Their skates drowned out the noise of distant traffic and a street sweeper several blocks away. The only sounds she heard echoing through the empty concrete canyon were the whoosh and bump of their rollers on the cement sidewalk and Sawyer's laughter as he pulled her along faster and faster.

Suddenly he gave a yank and let go of her. She squealed as the force sent her flying. With one arm she grabbed a lamp pole that materi-alized in front of her, and her momentum looped her around it twice before she stopped.

Sawyer, who had been laughing, took one look at her face and his laughter died. "Are you okay?"

Her eyes narrowed. "I'm going to get you for that."

His grin returned, and he took off in the opposite direction with Pip in hot pursuit. He obviously wasn't going at top speed, for she was soon able to overtake him. The rat even

made it easier by offering her his hand. She
took it in both of hers and whipped him as
hard as she could.

He only laughed, put his heels together and
went around and around in a circle. "You'll
have to do better than that, Short Stuff." He
stripped off his belt, threaded it through the
rear loop of his jeans, and secured it.

"What are you doing?"

"You'll see. Hang on to my belt and let's
fly."

With both hands she grabbed the looped
belt as he took off again. Faster and faster
he went, down the sidewalk, around corners.
All she could do was hunch over to avoid his
strides and hang on for dear life. So swiftly did
they move that she was sure that they would
be airborne at any moment. She squealed and
laughed and held on as he made dive-bombing
noises and flew down the curb ramp into the
street. In huge, sweeping arcs, he zigzagged
down the middle of Main, yelling like Tarzan.

It was exhilarating.

It was scary.

"Sawyer!" she shouted as the wind rushed
over her face. "Slow down."

He only laughed and skated faster as they
came to a corner.

Abruptly he bumped up a ramp to the sidewalk and stopped. She crashed into his back.

He let out a succinct oath. "You okay?"

"Other than the fact that my knees feel like rubber bands, I'm fine."

She let go of his belt and started to move forward. Reaching back, he clamped his arms together and kept her behind him as he skated her backward. "Get around the corner and find a dark doorway. Stay till I come for you. Go!"

Her heart almost stopped. Visions of muggers or gangs with guns and knives flashed through her mind. "Why?"

"The cops. Do it now."

She giggled. "I'm not falling for that gag again." She tried to shake loose.

"Dammit! This time I'm serious. Move."

"But I thought you said—"

"Now!" He gave her a shove.

Her heart went to her toes, but she moved. Images of being fingerprinted and tossed in jail put jets on her skates. She could see the headlines now.

At the first doorway she swung into the shadowed recess and plastered herself against a wall in the corner. Her breath came in great gasps as she waited for Sawyer.

He didn't come.

Trying to still her runaway heart with her splayed hand, she inched forward and peeked around the edge of the doorway.

Dear Lord, was he *crazy?*

There he was, at the corner half a block away, skating in lazy circles, swinging around lampposts, and singing at the top of his lungs. A police car was stopped nearby, and a uniformed officer was climbing from it.

She jerked her head back and plastered herself against the wall once more.

Oh . . . my . . . God . . .

For what seemed like an eternity she waited. And waited. And waited.

Screwing up her courage, she peered around the edge.

Nothing.

No police car. No policeman.

No Sawyer.

Oh . . . my . . . God . . .

Her back against the wall, she slowly slid down until her bottom touched the cement. She hugged her knees and dropped her forehead against them.

Stranded.

Sawyer was in jail; she was alone in downtown Houston, at two o'clock in the morning, with no transportation and not a penny to her name. She couldn't even call anybody to come pick her up.

There was nothing to do but wait until morning.

Nan would be frantic. Pip had neglected to leave a note.

She heard a car cruising slowly up the street. Her pulse raced. Painfully aware of her vulnerability, she refused to allow herself to consider the dire variety of horrendous possibilities. Still, her heart hammered.

The car stopped at the curb where she sat hunched in the dark corner. Her breath caught. Blood pounded in her ears.

"Hey, babe. Need a ride?"

She knew that voice. Her head jerked up. Her eyes narrowed; her lips thinned.

White-hot fury flashed through her as she scrambled to her feet and skated to the car. She yanked the door open and climbed inside.

"I may kill you," she said between clenched teeth. "Slowly and painfully."

He laughed. "Why? I thought it was a kick."

"I thought you'd been arrested! I thought I was stranded!"

"I'd never leave you stranded. And why would I be arrested?"

"Because of the police, you idiot!"

"We weren't doing anything illegal."

"Then why did he stop?"

Sawyer laughed. "He stopped to see if I was drunk."

"Drunk?"

"I guess he didn't appreciate my Gene Kelly imitation."

She frowned. "Who's Gene Kelly and what does he have to do with this?"

"Didn't you ever see the movie *Singing in the Rain*?"

"Sawyer," she said, exasperated, "you're not making sense."

He patiently explained that Gene Kelly was a dancer and described the famous scene in the movie where he sings and dances along the street. "I was doing my version on roller skates, but without the rain or the umbrella. He stopped to see if I was drunk."

"And?"

"Nothing on my breath but M&M's."

"If we weren't doing anything illegal, why did you have me hide?"

"Because we were acting kind of goofy, and when I saw the cop car, I figured he might

come to the conclusion that he did. I didn't
want you to be embarrassed."

"Oh."

"Sorry if I frightened you." He leaned over
and kissed her gently. "I thought I was being
gallant."

"You were. Thank you."

"Wanna skate some more?"

She rolled her eyes.

"Does that mean *no*?"

"Brilliant deduction."

"Hey, I'm no slouch in the IQ department
myself." He laughed as the sports car roared
down the empty street.

Sawyer drove barefoot, his helmet still on
his head with sprigs of hair sticking through the
holes. He was oddly endearing, Pip thought as
she removed her gear and changed into her
sneakers.

"You enjoyed that, didn't you?" she asked.
"Even the policeman."

He flashed his famous grin. "Yeah. I'm
pumped." He gave her thigh a quick pinch.
"You liked it too. Admit it."

She giggled. "It was kind of fun."

He slapped the steering wheel. "I knew it.
You're a closet daredevil. Careful. You have all
the makings of an adrenaline addict."

"Me? Not likely."

"We'll see. We'll see."

Later, after they pulled up at the lake house and got out, Pip said, "This time, let's use the front door."

"You got a key?"

"Oh, shoot."

"Up the tree. Come on. I'll give you a boost."

Even with Sawyer helping, climbing up was harder than climbing down.

Inside at last, she turned to find Sawyer straddling the tree limb, leaning with folded arms on the windowsill, his eyes dancing with merriment as usual.

"You had a blast, didn't you?" he asked.

She knelt by the window and gave him a kiss. "I had a blast."

He kissed her again, a longer, lingering kiss. "We're perfect together. Will you marry me, Short Stuff?"

She laughed. "Certainly not. Stop teasing."

He looked crestfallen, but she knew it was only an act. He sighed. "Well, if you won't marry me, will you at least fix me some breakfast? I'm starving."

"I'm not much of a cook, but I can probably manage some scrambled eggs."

"Great." He threw a leg over the sill and climbed in.

As it turned out, Sawyer fixed breakfast. French toast. Light on the cinnamon.

When he'd sopped his last piece with syrup and eaten it, he said, "Mind if I crash here? I'm bushed."

"Me too."

Arms around each other and with her head on his shoulder, they went upstairs. After a good-night kiss at her door, they parted, she to her room, he to the guest room.

Pip was tempted to linger with him, but she was so darned tired that she was almost asleep on her feet. As soon as she closed the door behind her, she stripped and fell into bed.

It seemed as if she'd barely closed her eyes and drifted off when someone was shaking her.

"Pip, wake up. I've got it," Sawyer said.

She mumbled into her pillow.

"What was that?"

"It can't be time to get up," she groaned. "It feels as if I just went to sleep."

"You did. It's only been ten minutes. Listen, I've thought of the perfect place for us to go."

"To go? *Now?*"

He laughed. "No, not now, Sleepyhead.

Tomorrow. I'll have to make arrangements. Pack a couple of bathing suits, some shorts, and a sexy dress. I'll be here bright and early tomorrow morning." He nuzzled her ear and stroked her back. "Where's your gown?"

She mumbled.

His lips trailed down her shoulder blade. "You're damned tempting. It's a good thing that I'm a person of high principles and an iron will."

She snorted.

"Go back to sleep, sweetheart. Get a *lot* of rest. Tomorrow's gonna be DFV-Day."

"Huh?"

"I'll explain later." He patted her bottom and kissed her cheek. "Go to sleep."

Before she drifted off again, she could have sworn that she heard him whisper, "*Je t'aime*, Short Stuff."

Pip balked at the steps of the small jet. "We're going *where*?"

"To Acapulco. Did you bring your bathing suit?"

She hoisted her small bag. "It's in here. But I don't even *own* a sexy dress."

"No problem. We'll buy one there." He

pulled her up the steps. "Ah, sun and sand, here we come."

"Who's flying this plane?"

"*Moi.*"

When she rolled her eyes and looked heavenward, he whipped out his wallet. "Want to see my credentials?"

"Is this jet *yours*?"

"Don't I wish. No, it's a loaner. Belongs to a friend of mine. Uncle Len would really blow a gasket if I bought a company plane. He thinks the chopper is bad enough. And truthfully I don't think Mirth could justify the cost of buying and maintaining a jet. But isn't she a honey?"

"Very nice."

Sawyer stowed their bags and led her to the cockpit. "Wanna be the copilot? Or the navigator?"

She glanced at all the dials and gauges. "I haven't the vaguest notion of what to do."

"I'll teach you. Quick as you are, you'll soon get the hang of it."

"Don't you think I should start smaller— like maybe with a prop plane? Anyhow, you forget that I have no sense of direction. If I navigate, we may end up in Pittsburgh."

"We're flying south." He helped her strap

in, then kissed her lightly. "Just relax and let me handle the flying. I've got everything under control." A devilish gleam sparked in his eyes. "And I mean *everything*."

Though she wasn't sure why, Pip felt slightly . . . jittery. And Sawyer's piloting abilities had nothing to do with her state. She had the beginnings of a headache, and her cheeks felt flushed.

Watching him buckle his seatbelt, a question popped into her mind. "I forgot to ask you about a term I'm not familiar with. What does DFV-Day mean?"

He winked, cocked a half-smile, and put on his headset. "Deflowering Virgin Day. Let's roll."

As they tootled up the hill in the little car with the striped canopy, Sawyer pointed out the beautiful surroundings and talked a mile a minute. He knew he was running off at the mouth, but, hell, he was so damned wired, he could hardly sit still. He was as horny as a twelve-point buck in mating season. And he had a lifetime supply of condoms in his bag. In all colors and shapes.

Slow and easy does it, he reminded himself for the hundredth time. He wanted this to be absolutely perfect for Pip. Memorable. Romantic.

And this was a gorgeous spot. They would be able to see the bay from their cottage—or *casita*, as it was called—and have their own private pool. He'd ordered a candlelight dinner to be served later. With champagne.

He'd thought of everything.

When he pulled to a stop at their door, he glanced at Pip. She was grimacing and rubbing her forehead.

"Honey, what's the matter?" he asked.

"I have a headache."

"Isn't it a little early in our relationship for that excuse?" She didn't reply. "You're joking, right?"

"There's nothing funny about the way my head feels. I think a little man inside is trying to chop his way out with an ax. Do you think we could find some aspirin?"

"Sure, sweetheart. Let me get the bags inside, and I'll run back down to the desk. Okay?"

She fluttered her hand.

Sawyer looked at her carefully and began to get nervous. He felt her forehead. "My God, Pip, you're burning up."

EIGHT

"Measles! I can't have measles," Pip whined. "Not now."

"I'm very sorry, *señora*, but I'm afraid such is the case," the doctor said. He patted her hand. "But don't despair. This variety only lasts for three days. We must keep you quarantined, but in two more days, then you can enjoy your honeymoon."

"But it's not—"

Sawyer cleared his throat. "Yes, uh, thank you, Doctor Martinez. *Gracias.*"

The two men left the bedroom.

"See that she gets plenty of rest, *señor,*" the gray-haired doctor said, eyeing Sawyer over the top of his glasses. "*Complete* rest. *No* vigorous activities. See that she drinks plenty of liquids." He handed Sawyer a vial. "And have her take one of these four times each day." Dr. Martinez cleared his throat. "Is it possible that she is with child?"

"Good God, no. She's a— No, it's not possible."

"*Bueno, bueno.* I had to ask. This can be a serious disease for expectant mothers." He patted Sawyer's shoulder. "Be very tender with her feelings. We men must be magnanimous about these things."

Sawyer was a little miffed when he closed the door behind the doctor. Hell, what did the guy take him for? He could be tender. Damned tender. He wasn't bent out of shape because Pip was sick. Her fever had scared him spitless.

He went back into the lavish bedroom of their cottage where she lay in bed, staring out the window at the bay and looking thoroughly miserable. Seeing her feel so terrible cut him to the quick. If he could have endured the headache and the fever for her, he would have done it in a flash. If he could have wiped the rash from her skin and spread it on his instead, he wouldn't have hesitated. But he couldn't.

And he felt so damned helpless.

She glanced up at him, her temperature making her pansy-colored eyes even brighter, and said, "Sawyer, I'm so sorry."

Her soulful expression tore his heart out.

He sat down on the bed beside her and gathered her into his arms. "Love, you have nothing to be sorry for. You probably caught the measles from Scooter, and it was my fault that you were exposed. I feel like a dirty dog."

She smiled and brushed an errant lock of hair from his forehead. It sprang back immediately. "How could you have known? It's no one's fault. I'm only sorry that I've spoiled our . . . vacation."

"Who says that it's spoiled? You'll be okay in a couple of days."

"But things will be so boring until then."

"*Boring?* Surely you jest. Don't you know that you're speaking with the world's expert on bedtime entertainment?" He grinned. "*Non*-vigorous entertainment, that is. I plan to take very good care of you." He frowned. "Unless you'd rather have Nan here. I could fly her down."

"No, Nan hates to fly. I just don't want to be a bother."

He kissed her nose. "Sweetheart, you could never be a bother." He gave her a pill, plumped her pillows, and settled her under the covers. "You take a nap now, and when you wake up, we'll have a sumptuous dinner in bed."

While she slept, Sawyer got busy on the phone. Before long a dozen deliveries were made to the door. For the things he couldn't find in Acapulco, he called Gloria, his secretary at Mirth. "Have someone take them to the airport immediately. Buy a seat on the plane if you have to. I want them here first thing in the morning."

"What are you doing in Acapulco?" Gloria asked.

"Playing Florence Nightingale for the moment. And don't tell anyone where I am. Especially Leonard."

"What about your mother? She's called twice today."

"I damned sure don't want my mother to know. Just tell anyone who asks that I'm out of the country on a project and you don't know when I'll return. You might hint that I'm in France. Or China. Hell, I don't care. Pick a place."

"How about Norway?"

"Why Norway?"

"I've always thought it would be a nice place to visit. All those tall, Viking types."

"Norway . . . Siberia . . . it doesn't matter. Just don't mention Mexico or Acapulco. Maybe you'd better take the package to the airport yourself so that we won't have a loose-lipped delivery man running around."

"No problem."

"And one more thing. I probably won't be back in time for the board of directors meeting. Tell Leonard that I want it postponed until next week."

"Next week. Got it, boss."

"Open up."

"Sawyer, I can feed myself!"

Sawyer, who was sitting cross-legged in the middle of the king-size bed and wearing only running shorts and a faded green T-shirt, ignored her protests. He dipped from the bowl he held and offered the spoon to her lips. "*VROOM, VROOM.* Here comes the Batmobile. Open the bat cave. *VROOM, VROOM.*"

A snort of laughter burst from Pip. "The *Batmobile*?"

He grinned. "It always worked with me."

"Why must I have chicken soup? I'd rather have some of the lobster and asparagus." She pointed to the beautifully appointed cart beside her bed. "And that fruit looks luscious."

"Let's see how you do with the soup first. Everybody knows that chicken soup is very therapeutic. In my lifetime I've eaten gallons and gallons of the stuff."

"Then why aren't you having some?"

"I *hate* chicken soup. Open up."

After a few more sips he set the bowl aside. "How's your tummy?"

"Except for the rash *outside*, my tummy's fine. Now may I have some lobster?"

"Sure. I'll cut it for you."

"*Sawyer!*"

"You don't want me to cut it for you?" He looked as woebegone as a kicked puppy.

She touched his cheek. Hurting his feelings was the last thing she wanted to do. He had been completely, maddeningly solicitous of her since their arrival. And while she napped, he obviously had been busy. Every available surface was covered with lush flower arrangements. A dozen soft gowns, robes, and bed wraps had materialized as well as a VCR and tapes, a chess set, a Scrabble game, and a deck of cards.

"You're being a dear about this, and I

appreciate it more than I can say, but why don't we eat *together*? I'm not so ill that I can't manage to cut my food and feed myself."

"Great." He grinned. "You wanna feed me?"

Plucking a grape from the fruit bowl, she held it to his lips.

"*What?*" Looking aghast, he drew back. "You aren't going to peel it first?"

Laughing, she threw it at him. He caught it and popped it into his mouth.

With only a minimal amount of hovering by Sawyer, they finished their meal.

Sawyer stacked the dishes on the cart and wheeled it into the suite's living room. When he returned, he rubbed his hands together. "What'll it be? Chess? Scrabble? Gin rummy? How about a movie?"

"A movie sounds nice. What are the choices?"

He smiled slyly. "Would you believe that I found *Singing in the Rain*?"

"The one with Gene Kelly?"

"Yep. The very one." He waved a tape in the air, then slid it into the VCR. When everything was set, he climbed into bed next to her, stacked pillows behind him, and settled back. "You're going to love it." He held out the remote control and gave it a flick. The screen came to life.

After a few moments Sawyer sat up and spat out a disgusted oath. "The damned thing's in *Spanish*."

Pip bit back a giggle. "Naturally. We're in Mexico."

"But— Oh, that's right. You speak Spanish, don't you?"

She nodded.

He smiled and settled again into his place beside her. "That's okay, then. I know most of the lines by heart. The ones I've forgotten, you can translate."

Pip's eyes popped open. She couldn't turn. She couldn't move. She was being held down by a weight across her legs and another across her upper body. Instinctively she let out a shriek and began churning to free herself.

Wild-eyed, Sawyer jumped out of bed, turned on the light, and yelled, "What's wrong? What's wrong? Are you in pain?"

When she realized that he had been the source of the weight, she relaxed against the pillows, but her heart continued to race.

She fluttered her hand. "I'm fine now, but you frightened me. What are you doing in my bed?"

"I *was* sleeping. Do you need another pill?"

"No. I thought there was another bedroom."

"There is. But I'm sleeping here. You might need something."

"But—"

"No *but*s. I'm staying right here. If you're feeling modest, forget it. In a couple of more days there won't be any room for modesty anyway." He tucked the covers under her chin, turned off the light, and lay down beside her, atop the spread.

"Sawyer, aren't you cold?"

"Not likely."

"Why don't you at least get under the covers with me."

"Not on your life. Not for two more days. Then you can't keep me out."

They were quiet for a moment. The distant sound of the surf washed through the silence. The sweet scent of flowers and the subtle crackle of sexual tension filled the air. She rolled onto her side, away from him.

"Sawyer?"

"Hmmm?"

"Did you know that you're the best friend I ever had?"

He snuggled against her, spoon fashion. "You're my best friend too."

"I am?"

"Yep."

"Sawyer?"

"Hmmm?"

"I'm a little nervous about—you know."

"Nothing to be nervous about. It's just me. You're having typical bride's jitters."

"But I'm not a bride."

His voice sounded hoarse when he replied, "We could remedy that easily enough."

"Oh, Sawyer, don't tease. I'm nervous because I'm afraid I'll disappoint you."

"Not a chance. Trust me. Now, go to sleep."

When her breathing slowed, Sawyer got up and took a cold shower. He took another one the next morning. He discovered that cold showers didn't help a damned bit. He wanted her so badly—and not only sexually, though he was damned horny—he wanted her for keeps.

Why was it that every time he brought up marriage, she sidestepped the issue? Did she really think he was kidding? He wasn't. He was dead serious. What would it take to convince her? He'd try to think of something spectacular.

He'd rent a huge billboard. Naw, that had been overdone. He considered and discarded one idea after the other as he pushed their lunch cart into the bedroom.

"What are you thinking about so intensely?"

He grinned. "About you. About blimps and skywriters." He took the silver cover off a plate and inhaled the food's aroma. "About roast beef." He tucked a napkin in her robe. "I hope you like it rare."

After the doctor left, having pronounced Pip almost well, she and Sawyer sat at the dining table playing one of the games Gloria had sent. "I'll be glad to get out of here tomorrow and see some of the sights," Pip said.

"Not tomorrow. He said you'd be well by tomorrow but to stay out of the sun for another day."

"Spoilsport."

"You don't want to relapse, do you? I sure as hell don't want you to."

She touched his hand. "This has been very hard on you, hasn't it?"

He cocked an eyebrow, and a slow grin lifted one side of his mouth. "It's been hard, all right."

"Oh, *Sawyer*." She giggled. "It's your move."

"Not until tomorrow."

"The game! The game!"

"Oh, yeah." He threw the dice and advanced his token.

"This is a wonderful board game," she said. "Did you really invent it?"

"Yep. It was one of my first. And still our biggest seller. It and a couple of others are the backbone of the company."

"How many games have you invented?"

"Oh, I don't know. Including the computer games, I guess about twenty or so. I try to come up with a new one every year."

They finished the game, and after the sun had set, they lounged on the patio and sipped fruit drinks. Sawyer even consented to allow her to sit beside the pool and dip her feet in the water, where a score of hibiscus blossoms floated.

"It's so beautiful here," she said, holding her face to the sea breeze.

"*You* make it beautiful." Cupping her face in his hands, he kissed her gently.

Her arms went around him, and she tried to deepen the kiss, but he pulled away. "But, Sawyer—"

"After tomorrow I'll be a kissing fool, but not until then."

She reached down and dashed a spray of pool water on him. "You're making me crazy."

He laughed. "Join the club."

Sawyer did allow her to venture out the following day, but only by taxi to drive around the city and see the scenery and to visit the covered markets and pricey boutiques. Any time they went from taxi to building, he insisted on shading her with a giant red-and-white golf umbrella. She felt a little foolish, but at the same time . . . cherished.

He wouldn't be satisfied until he'd bought her two pretty, and very sexy, dresses. The black one was a lined gossamer batiste with tiny straps and with delicate lace edging the handkerchief hem. The other was silk and the color of her eyes. He would have bought her a dozen more if she would have allowed it. And accessories to go with them. As it was, the taxi seat was heaped with packages by the time they returned to the hotel.

Sawyer shaded her with the umbrella until they reached the portico, then helped her inside and instructed her to wait while he and the taxi driver unloaded their purchases.

Pip sat on the cushy white couch, took off her sneakers, and propped her heels on the coffee table. When the bags and boxes were stowed in the bedroom, Sawyer joined her in the living room and fixed a pair of frosty fruit drinks.

He handed one to her. She took a sip. "Ahhh, heaven. Thanks."

"Tired?" he asked as he wiggled her big toe. He dropped down beside her.

"Pooped."

"After you finish your drink, you need to take a nap. Then you can have a nice bubble bath and get ready for our night out."

"Where are we going?"

He kissed her shoulder. "It's a surprise. But I promise you a very romantic evening." He picked up her braid and tickled her nose with the end. "You ever wear your hair loose?"

"Not very often."

He kissed the cap of her shoulder again and

made a small circle with his tongue. "Wear it loose tonight. For me."

She swallowed hard. "All right."

"While you nap and dress, I'll use the other bedroom. I have a couple of errands and some arrangements to make."

Sawyer had tied the blasted tie three times before it looked right. And no amount of blow-drying and brushing could tame his unruly hair, but he gave it his best shot. He wanted tonight to be perfect.

Damn, he was nervous. He felt like a bride-groom on his wedding night. And truthfully, as far as he was concerned, it was their wedding night. Oh, he didn't plan to mess up things by pressing the marriage issue tonight, but before they left Acapulco, he planned to.

He gave his shoes a final buffing, put on his jacket, and checked his reflection in the full-length mirror. He knew that he wasn't as handsome a man as Pip deserved—he grinned—but she couldn't find another one in the solar system who loved her any more.

Taking a deep breath, he squared his shoulders and went into the living room to wait.

A few minutes later, Pip's door opened, and she came out. His breath left him. He felt as if he'd been whacked in the head by a two-by-four.

She was gorgeous.

The sides of her hair were caught in a bunch of curls on her crown, and the rest of it fell down to her waist in gentle waves. With her makeup and that sexy black dress, she looked like a movie star.

She glanced down as herself, then up at him. "Do I look okay?" she asked, touching the orchid he'd sent that was nestled in the crown of curls.

"Turn around."

As she turned in the strappy sandals on her dainty feet, his eyes devoured her from top to bottom.

"No, not okay," he said. "Beautiful. Lovely. Exquisite . . . Words fail me."

She smiled. "You look very handsome in your suit." She touched the flower in her hair. "Thank you for the orchid."

"I wanted to match your eyes, but it's a shade off. Sorry about that."

Drawing near, she tiptoed to kiss his cheek. "It's perfect." She held up the matching wrap draped over her arm. "Will I need this?"

"It's warm outside now, but it may get cool later."

Outside, a white limousine waited, the uniformed driver beside the door. Pip laughed as they climbed inside. "I feel like Cinderella."

Sawyer kissed her hand. "There are some major differences. I'm no Prince Charming. You're not wearing glass slippers. And at midnight I'll be right beside you. And at one o'clock. And two. And three. And . . ."

They sat in a private alcove high above the bay. Soft guitars strummed in the background. Open French doors admitted the sound of the surf dashing against the cliff below. Bougainvillea, blooming in great rosy clusters, draped the balustrade of the small balcony just outside the doors. A gentle breeze, fresh and salty, stirred the flames of the candles, sending dancing light and shadow across the stucco walls and over the pristine tablecloth, striking the crystal champagne glasses, and the tiny bubbles rising inside, with multicolored sparks.

"Oh, Sawyer, this place is lovely. And dinner was . . . divine. However did you find this restaurant?"

"The hotel's concierge and I have become

fast friends. He said it was the most romantic spot in the city."

A guitarist strolled by and stopped to serenade them with a soft love song. They held hands and sipped champagne while they listened.

When the musician moved on, Sawyer asked, "Would you like to go into the lounge and dance for a while?"

She brightened. "Could we? I'd like to try some of the dances you've taught me with a real Latin band."

As they came through the door of their cottage, Pip was laughing, and Sawyer was holding a champagne bottle and two fluted glasses high in the air.

"One, two, cha-cha-cha," he chanted, bumping Pip's hip with his. "We're a pair of dancing fools. Move over, Fred and Ginger—here we come."

"Who are Fred and Ginger?"

"Oh, don't tell me!" he groaned theatrically, draping his arms over her shoulders. "Everybody has heard of Fred and Ginger. When I was a kid, I learned to dance watching their old movies."

"How could you learn to dance by watching movies? I thought you weren't allowed out of bed."

He brushed his lips over her hairline. "In my head, sweetheart. In my head, sweetheart. In my head. The same way I've—"

"What?"

"Never mind. Want some more champagne?"

She shook her head and lifted her face to him. "Are you nervous?"

He laughed. "*Moi?* Nervous? Why should I be nervous? Just because I'm about to become your first lover, and I've never had a virgin, and I may screw it up—excuse me, bad choice of words—so that I may do something wrong and hurt you and traumatize you forever? Why should I be nervous?"

Chuckling, she divested him of the bottle and glasses, then wrapped her arms around his waist and laid her head against his chest. "I trust you implicitly."

He gathered her close and rubbed his cheek across her forehead. "Oh, Pip, honey, I love you so."

"You do?"

"I do."

She lifted her face to him, and gently, oh,

so gently, he touched her lips with his. His mouth was warm and moist, and he smelled of champagne and cherries and chocolate.

His tongue sought entry, and she opened to him, reveling in the taste and texture. The kiss deepened, and he cupped her bottom, drawing her closer against his hardness. She trembled in his arms, and she could feel his body trembling as well.

She broke away and, taking him by the hand, said, "Come."

"Love, we don't have to rush this. Let's take it slow and easy. We need to make sure you're ready."

Beguilingly, she smiled over her shoulder. "I'm ready." She kicked off her sandals.

He kicked off his shoes. On the way to the bedroom he shed his jacket and tie, jerked his shirt out, and had half the buttons undone by the time they reached the big bed, where a fat candle flickered nearby.

"Let me," she said, brushing his hands away and finishing the buttons.

While she worked, he trailed kisses down her neck and along her shoulders, lowering the thin straps as he went. As her hands made slow, sweeping circles over his chest, he found the zipper at her back and pulled it down, unhooked her bra, and helped her strip her garments away until she was left in only earrings and a black scrap of lace.

His hands slipped over every inch of her skin within his reach. "I love the way you feel. Here. And here. And here." He lifted her and laid her on the bed, his eyes seeming to feast on her as he undressed.

Leaving on his dark briefs, he joined her, kissing his way up from her toes to her mouth. He gathered her hair in his hands and rubbed his face in its thickness. "I love your hair," he whispered. "The way it looks, the way it smells, the way it feels. Like black silk."

He let the long strands sift through his fingers over her breasts, then parted the dark curtain to make way for his lips, his teeth, his tongue. He laved her every surface, praising each place as he passed. His touch, gentle as a fairy's wing, his murmurs, soft as a clover leaf, turned her blood to fire.

His tongue dipped into her navel. Her stomach contracted, and she threaded her fingers through his hair. "I want you," she whispered.

"Soon, love."

But it seemed forever that he worked his magic on her body. Under his touch she turned to liquid moonlight shimmering on a sea of sensation. A desperate yearning filled her, swelled her, sent sweet aches coursing deep inside.

When he slipped off her panties and his briefs, rolled on a condom, and knelt between her legs, she reached for him. "Not yet, love. Lie back."

His fingers lightly stroked the insides of her thighs, and her back arched. He bent, and his lips and tongue followed the path to the juncture of her legs toward the site of her yearning.

When she felt the thrust of his tongue, her eyes widened, and she grabbed handfuls of his hair. "What are you *doing*?"

Candlelight danced in his green eyes as he glanced up at her from his ministrations. "Loving you."

"But— But— I don't think you're supposed to do it that way."

He laughed, and the sound vibrated against her skin, heightening the sensation even more. "Does it feel good?" His tongue made another foray.

"Dear Lord . . . yessss."

"Then it's the right way."

Awash in sensation, she could only strain toward the source of her pleasure. A fine sheen of perspiration broke over her skin. When his teeth touched her, she went wild. When his fingers probed deeply, she went wilder.

"Easy, love." He lifted her hips slightly and moved against her ever so gently.

She ached for the fullness that barely entered her, reached instinctively for him, begging to be filled. His mouth moved to hers, and she kissed him hungrily, clung to him, eager for . . . something.

When he didn't move his lower body, she did. She wrapped her legs around his hips, pulling him into her and thrusting herself upward against him.

In a moment of pain she yelped.

He went dead still. "Oh, my God. I've hurt you."

"Who cares? Do something. I'm dying."

He slipped his hand between them and stroked a sensitive spot that sent her into a frenzy. Sensation built and built until she was sure she could stand no more. Pleasure and agony and reaching. Reaching.

Suddenly the most potent sense of ecstasy burst over her like a meteor shower. Her body convulsed, and ripples of bliss went on and on and on. He held her close as she drowned in heady sensation. She felt his sweat-slicked body tremble under her hands and felt him throb inside her.

A low groan escaped from deep in his throat.

For long moments they were silent, still joined, as the candle flickered and the wax dripped slowly down the side.

"Sawyer?"

"Hmmm."

"I think I'm going to like this."

He laughed. "It gets better."

NINE

Holding hands and laughing, they ran into the sparkling surf, hopping small white-capped waves, then diving into larger ones. They frolicked in the azure water like young dolphins at play, chasing each other, playing tag beneath the surface, dunking, spraying, laughing. Always laughing.

Hands entwined, they floated on the salty blue bay while Sawyer tried to teach her to spit water like a geyser. They watched lacy clouds overhead and marveled at the beauty of the cliffs and inlets.

After a time they swam to shore. Pip dried off with a towel, but Sawyer shook himself like a dog, spraying water on her. Squealing, she ducked and shielded herself with her hands. "Stop that!" Snatching up her towel, she snapped his bottom with it.

"I should have never taught you that trick," he said, dancing out of her reach. He plucked a bottle from her bag. "Here, let me put some more sunscreen on you."

"I'm covered with three coats of the stuff now."

Undeterred, he began slathering lotion on her body. "Some probably got washed off in the water. Turn around."

"You're a bigger worrywart than Nan."

He nipped her neck. "Yes, but you love it. Admit it."

She smiled, admitting nothing. The past two days—and nights—had been glorious, enchanting. Magical.

Once she'd been initiated into the delights of lovemaking, she reveled in it. Sawyer was a wonderful lover—tender, yet demanding. Considerate. Inventive. And she was a quick study. Of course her previous reading on the subject had helped significantly.

And besides making love for hours, they'd had fun doing other things as well. Sawyer had insisted on seeing the spot where many of the Tarzan movies were filmed. "But he was my *hero*," he explained when she didn't see anything profound about tramping through the cove's undergrowth. "Cheetah must have stood right here."

"Cheetah?"

"You know, *Cheetah*." He made monkey sounds and scratched his sides. "He was a chimp." When she looked blank, he said, "We'll add Tarzan movies to the list."

They'd wandered through the noisy marketplace, dodging playful children and buying paper flowers, sandals, and serapes. They bought huaraches that smelled of new leather and creaked when they walked in them. They'd bargained for several gaily embroidered dresses for Nan and Mrs. Tinker, an exquisitely carved onyx chess set for her uncles, and a silver belt for Gloria.

And of course Sawyer bought a sombrero, the biggest and gaudiest one he could find. Red with an abundance of rhinestones and spangles.

After some spirited dickering, which Sawyer enjoyed thoroughly, he loaded Pip down with jewelry—a dozen silver bracelets for each of her arms, rings for every finger, and combs for her hair. He'd even insisted on buying a huge papier-mâché mushroom in fanciful shades of pink, decorated with painted flowers and with a winged fairy sitting on top.

The evening before, they'd sipped creamy rum drinks by torchlight and watched cliff divers plunge from high precipices into dangerous water several stories below. She'd had to physically restrain Sawyer from climbing up and trying it himself. Afterward they'd returned to their cottage and made love. Vigorously.

She smiled.

"You look like the cat that ate the canary," Sawyer said. "What are you thinking about?"

"Cliff divers."

They joined hands and strolled down the beach. The fine sand at the water's edge was cool beneath her feet, the sun warm on her back. The stiff breeze soon dried the loose tendrils around her hairline and sent them whipping across her face.

A flutter of color caught her eye, and she shaded her brow to see better. "Oh, look!"

Farther down the beach, a Jeep pulled a gaily striped gilder that sailed its rider high over the water.

"You ever tried hang gliding?" Sawyer asked.

She shook her head.

"It's fantastic. Lots better than flying off your uncle's car with a tablecloth." Chuckling, he hooked his arm around her neck and kissed her forehead. "If you'd like, we'll go to California sometime, and I'll teach you the real thing." With his head, he gestured toward the Jeep. "In the meantime this is a good start. Want to try it?"

"Why not? If I break my neck, will you take me to the hospital?"

He grinned. "And stay by your side and feed you chicken soup. But you're not going to break your neck. Come on. You're gonna love it."

She did.

Flying high above the water with the wind rushing past her face and snapping the bright-hued fabric, she laughed spontaneously. Totally exhilarated, she felt like a bird soaring free from earth's gravity. It was a thrill, an awesome invigoration of her senses rivaled only by making love with Sawyer.

It was . . . magic.

And extremely stimulating.

When the ride was over, she ran, laughing, into Sawyer's arms. He swung her around and kissed her, much to the delight of the young men providing the gliding service, if their laughter and comments were any indication. She ignored their slightly suggestive remarks. She felt like making a few herself.

"I don't have to ask if you enjoyed the ride." Sawyer said.

She grinned. "It was a kick."

He hugged her to his side. "Wanna go take a nap?"

"A *nap*?"

A knowing smile spread over his face. "A polite euphemism."

She gave an exaggerated yawn. "I'm suddenly very sleepy."

He threw back his head and laughed. "Like hell you are. You're pumped to the gills. I know the feeling. Come on."

Pip came slowly awake, stretching. When her eyes opened, Sawyer lay beside her, his head propped in his hand, his gaze on her.

She smiled. "I really did take a nap."

"I noticed."

"Did you?"

"Uh-uh. I watched you. Hungry? Lunch just came. It's on the patio."

She quickly donned a short robe, and with

Sawyer clad only in shorts they strolled to their private patio with its small pool. They dined on black bean soup, huge fat shrimp, and an assortment of luscious melon.

"Ah," she said, lazing back in her padded chaise and nibbling a slice of cantaloupe she held in her fingers, "this is the life. It's a shame we can't go on this way forever."

He leaned over and gobbled the last of the melon from her hand and licked the sweet juice from her fingers. "Why can't we?"

"Don't be silly. Eventually we have to go home. My leave of absence isn't permanent, you know. I have work to do, work that requires long hours and meticulous attention."

"Come to work for Mirth on the virtual reality project." He winked. "I know the boss. He'll give you all the time off you want."

Her heart lurched. "Is it important to you that I come to work for your company?"

"Only if you would enjoy it. Only if it would make you happy. Your happiness is my number-one concern." He stood and held out his hand to her. "Let's go for a dip in our pool."

She rose and turned to go inside.

"Where are you going?"

"To put on my bathing suit."

"Why?" He reached for the belt of her robe. "Haven't you ever been skinny-dipping?"

She shook her head.

Slowly he unbraided her hair.

Her robe fell to the ground. His shorts followed.

She stepped into the pool. He followed.

Scooping up one of the red blossoms that floated on the water, he moved toward her and tucked the flower over her ear. "Have I told you how exquisite you are?"

She smiled. "Many times. But tell me again. I love to hear it."

"You are. Your ears—" He traced the outline of the one where the flower was tucked.

"*Les esgourdes*," she said.

"Your eyes." He kissed each lid.

"*Les mirettes.*"

"Your lips."

"*Les babines.*"

"*Les babines,*" he repeated as his mouth brushed hers. His hand dipped below the water. "And this?"

She whispered in his ear.

"Sounds naughty."

"Ohhh, it is."

❦———————❦

They were about to step into the shower when the phone rang. "I'll get it," Sawyer said. "Go ahead."

The voice on the other end of the line wasn't one Sawyer expected to hear. "How in the hell did you find me?"

"It wasn't easy," Herb Burkhalter said. "I had to twist Gloria's arm, then call half the hotels in Acapulco. We have problems here, my friend. Big problems."

When Herb explained the situation, Sawyer's frown disintegrated into a scowl. "That bastard! I'll be back tonight. Can you meet me at my house at eight for a strategy session? Tell Gloria to be there too. And the company attorney."

When he hung up, Sawyer cursed loud and long, then jerked up the phone and called the concierge. "Cancel the mariachis. Cancel the fireworks. We have an emergency and must leave immediately. Could you call the airport and have them see that my plane is ready for takeoff in an hour? Yes, a taxi, please. Thank you."

Pip touched his arm. Her eyes were troubled. "What's wrong?"

He hugged her tight. "Oh, sweetheart. Dammit, we have to leave. And I had such plans for tonight. Big plans. But Leonard Hooker, that sneaky son-of-a-bitch, didn't postpone the board of directors meeting like I told him to. It's still on for tomorrow morning. And my mother is in Houston, nosing around the office."

"I don't understand."

"I wish I didn't. My mother *never* comes to board meetings. I always vote her stock."

"Explain, please."

"I don't have time to go into all of it now, but what it boils down to is that if my mother aligns herself with my uncle, they have control of Mirth. Rather, Leonard has control."

"But it's *your* company. Surely they wouldn't—"

"They damned well might. Especially if I'm not there to explain things to my mother."

"Would your uncle do such an underhanded thing?"

"I wouldn't have thought so, but it looks damned suspicious." He lifted her chin and kissed her. "Do you mind that we have to leave?"

"Of course not. We're going back and show that . . . that old pirate a thing or two. Take over indeed! We won't allow it! Why, he would have those boys at the ranch out on the street by sundown. Let's pack."

As she stalked across the room and grabbed her suitcase, Sawyer watched her and grinned. "I've said it before, but, Short Stuff, you're some kind of woman."

"And what kind is that?" she asked with a saucy bobble of her head.

He laughed. "My kind."

By midnight everyone had left, and Sawyer and Pip stood on the deck at Sawyer's house. Arms around each other, they gazed through the trees at the full moon. Its light was so bright that the wildflowers on the knoll glistened an eerie silver-blue.

"Don't worry," Pip said. "That old reprobate doesn't stand a chance. You'll see."

"I hope you're right. And thanks for asking your brother to sit in on the meeting. He was a big help. And a nice guy."

"He is nice. And John's a whiz with business problems. A genius really."

"Genius must run in your family."

She sighed. "I suppose. Uncle Waldo and Uncle Emory would have been glad to contribute to the strategy session, but they tend to get bogged down in the theoretical aspects. John is very practical. He liked you, you know."

"I'm glad."

"He said I really should take the consultant's job on the virtual reality project."

"He *is* a genius. Are you going to?"

"We'll see. I need some time to process and evaluate some personal things first."

"What things?" Sawyer asked. Secretly he hoped that he was the major part of those "personal things."

"My project. My program for *Accelerated Remediation of Social Development*. Had you forgotten?"

He wanted to laugh, but she looked so serious that he didn't dare. He cleared his throat. "I confess that it had slipped my mind. Are you still working on that?"

"Why, certainly. Isn't that what we've been doing?"

A chuckle slipped out. "I suppose you could call it that. You about ready to turn in?"

"Are you sleepy?"

"No, I'm still pretty wired, but a *nap* might help."

She smiled. "Euphemisms again?"

"Mmm-hmmm," he murmured as his lips met hers.

————⬧————

Pip and Sawyer sat in his office listening through the intercom Gloria had rigged in the board room next door. Dressed in a tailored suit and with her hair wound into a neat coil at her crown, Pip sat on the edge of her chair. Sawyer, decked out in his usual jeans, polo shirt, and scruffy sport shoes, sat reared back with his feet propped on his desk and his fingers laced across his abdomen.

"Coffee, Captain Hooker?" they heard Gloria say sweetly.

"Er, uh, fine, thank you." After a pause Leonard said, "Are we all here?"

"Everyone except Sawyer . . . you remember him," Herb noted. "Our *president. Chairman* of the board."

"Well, er, uh, our chairman is out of the country. In Norway, I believe. Can't for the life of me understand why he'd be in Norway." Hooker cleared his throat. "But he opted to ignore this very important quarterly board meeting. In his absence I'll preside." A gavel banged. "Will the meeting please come to order."

Sawyer snickered, and, in an aside to Pip,

said, "Wonder where he got the gavel? I usually clink my water glass with a spoon."

"Shhh. I want to hear this."

"The first item on the agenda is the quarterly report. Gloria, would you put up the chart, please?" After some shuffling, Hooker continued. "As you can see, our profits are down ten percent from last quarter, which were down ten percent from the quarter before. Mr. Burkhalter, could you tell us why?"

"Len, er, Captain Hooker, as you very well know, initial expenditures on our new virtual reality projects were very high, but—"

"I see. And who is in charge of these projects?"

"Well, I suppose you could say that Sawyer is, but—"

"I see. And has he been actively involved in these projects in the past few weeks?"

"Well, no. Not exactly, but he has plans."

Hooker cleared his throat. "He has *plans*." Sarcasm dripped from his words. "But has he *done* anything? Is the program moving along?"

This time Herb cleared his throat. "He's working on it. We're stalled until we can add an expert in the field to . . ."

Pip looked sharply at Sawyer. Her eyes narrowed.

Sawyer's feet hit the floor. "Honey, it's not what you think."

"And how do you know what I think?"

"Because—" He raked his fingers through his hair. "Oh, hell, I'll explain later. Trust me, will you."

"Shhh, listen."

" . . . view of these developments, I'm proposing that the board remove Sawyer Hayes as president and chairman of the board."

"And replace him with whom?" Herb asked.

"Er, uh, since I'm next in command, I suppose I should take over the helm." He cleared his throat. "For the good of the company of course. All those in favor?"

There were only two ayes, but Madeline Hayes and Leonard Hooker together held the majority of the stock.

"That's our cue," Sawyer said.

They rose and went into the board room.

"Morning, everybody," Sawyer said, smiling as he strolled to the long table and nodded to each of those sitting around it. "Sorry we're late. Hello, Mother."

He bent and kissed his mother's cheek. Madeline Hayes, dressed in a pink suit with a lace jabot, smiled up at her son. Her hair, a graying version of Sawyer's, was coaxed into an updo that showed off the large pearl-and-diamond earrings she wore.

"Sawyer!" Madeline said. "Where on earth have you been? I've been trying to reach you for days. Len told me—"

"Sorry, Mother, that I couldn't be reached. Been in high-level negotiations. I'd like for you to meet Dr. Marguerite LeBaron, one of the country's leading experts in the field of virtual reality. She's agreed to come aboard."

Pip offered her hand to the older woman. Smiling graciously, Madeline clasped Pip's hand in both of hers. "I'm delighted to meet you, Dr. LeBaron."

"And I you, Mrs. Hayes. From what I've seen of the virtual reality program, it promises to be very exciting, a real coup for Mirth. They are a vanguard in the industry."

Madeline fluttered her fingers in her jabot. "And what does that mean for the stockholders, dear?"

Pip smiled. "It means that you're going to make lots of money."

Madeline beamed. "My son is an absolute genius." She patted him. "That's why I've always let him handle everything for me."

Grinning, Sawyer sauntered to the head

of the table, where Hooker stood scowling. "How's tricks, Uncle Len?" He plucked the gavel from his uncle's hand. "Thanks for taking over for me."

Hooker wrestled the gavel from Sawyer. "We've just voted you out. I'm in charge now."

Sawyer's eyebrows went up. "Oh?" He glanced at Pip. "I'll bet if Dr. LeBaron knew that, she'd refuse the consultancy." Pip nodded.

"We can find another consultant," Hooker blustered.

"And how long do you think the company can stay afloat if I withdraw permission to use my patents and copyrights?"

"*Your* patents and copyrights?"

"A good many of the games and other products that we manufacture, *I* created. They account for most of our profit, and they're mine, not Mirth's." He gestured with his head toward the company attorney. "Ask Preston."

Hooker's eyes darted to the attorney, who nodded. "Surely you wouldn't withdraw—"

"In a flash." Sawyer's voice was cold. "If you boot me out, you'll be president of a company that will be bankrupt before the end of next week."

Madeline gasped.

Sawyer turned to her. "Mother, would you like to change your vote?"

"I most certainly would. My son should remain in charge, as always."

"I'm with you." Sawyer glanced around the room. "Any further business?"

Silence.

He yanked the gavel from Hooker's clenched fist and banged it on the table. "The meeting is adjourned." Turning his back to the group, he addressed his uncle in a low, but firm voice. "You have one hour to have your resignation on my desk and your personal things cleared out of the building."

Pip managed to endure lunch with Sawyer and his mother without confronting Sawyer about his reasons for courting her so avidly. But all sorts of questions formed in her head. They ate at Vargo's, one of her favorite places, but neither the beautiful grounds of the garden-house setting nor the peacocks strolling under the trees distracted her from her ruminations.

With only half an ear she listened to Madeline Hayes prattle on about her redecorating projects, her committee work, and her bridge club in Florida. Pip couldn't imagine spending her life flitting around with no purpose of any consequence. Madeline was a vain, shallow woman with no substance that Pip could discern. Her only redeeming feature was that she did seem to care deeply for Sawyer in her own frivolous way.

Yet Pip couldn't forgive her for making a child endure years in bed when he should have been leading a normal life. Knowing their history and being around Madeline, she could understand why Sawyer avoided his mother as much as possible. It would probably take a psychologist years to unravel the dynamics involved. Pip was no psychologist.

Nor was she interested in Madeline Hayes or how she squandered her time. She *was* interested in Sawyer. They had serious issues to discuss.

The tedious lunch seemed interminable.

The meal finally over, Madeline insisted on strolling through the grounds, oohing and aahing over every bush and tree, emphasizing her gushing pronouncements with a flourish of the peacock feather she'd found on the path.

Pip appreciated the loveliness of nature as much as anyone, but enough was enough.

When Madeline stopped to sniff a flowering vine and eloquently extol its properties, Sawyer whispered to Pip, "Sorry about this. I'll get rid of her as soon as I can."

Trying to be a good sport, Pip smiled feebly. "We have to talk," she whispered.

"Later."

If she hadn't known that Sawyer was probably as miserable in his mother's company as she was, she might have accused him of delaying tactics.

They accompanied Madeline to her suite at the Warwick and waited while she flitted around getting packed for her trip to the airport. And they couldn't simply drop her off. Madeline insisted that they join her for a drink in the airline club while she waited.

While they drove to the lake house from the airport, Sawyer chattered like a magpie. Pip had come to know him well enough to observe that when he was nervous, he talked. She wanted to discuss some serious issues, but she couldn't get a word in. During the trip he recounted an entire John Wayne movie, complete with drawls, accents, and sound effects.

And try as she might to be irritated with

him, she could only laugh. Sawyer was always entertaining.

At the front door of the house, Pip said, "Wait for me while I change. Then, we're going to talk."

"But we *have* been talking."

"No. You've been talking. And I've been listening to a complete movie plot."

He looked wounded. "You didn't like my version of *Rio Bravo*?"

How could she offend one who oozed such endearing charm? She smiled and touched his cheek. "Your enactment of *Rio Bravo* was smashing. But we still need to talk."

"About what?"

"Later. Wait here," she instructed, but when she went inside, he followed.

"Where are you going?"

"With you. To help you change." He yawned. "I could use a nap too."

"Not now. And not with Nan in the house. She's old-fashioned." She backed him to a chair and shoved him down into it. "Wait here."

He gave her a jaunty salute. "With bated breath."

TEN

The sun drifted low over the lake as Pip and Sawyer strolled toward the pier where the houseboat was moored. He reached down and scooped up a handful of pebbles as they walked. The scent of hickory smoke from a barbecue grill somewhere across the way wafted over the lazy current. Insects skimmed the surface that lapped gently from the wake of a distant boat pulling a water-skier.

"You ever done any water-skiing?" he asked.

"Yes. The Strahan twins taught me. I think I was too inhibited at the time to be much good at it."

"Think you'd be better now?"

She stopped and looked intently at him as she considered the question. "Yes. Yes, I think I would be. It occurs to me that I've learned that from you. Being less inhibited, I mean."

Sawyer, with one hand in his pocket and the other shaking the pebbles, ambled beside her as she continued to walk along the wooden planks of the pier. "Though it hasn't been very long, it seems as if a lifetime has passed since I first walked down this pier and saw you standing there in those funny glasses with paint dribbling on your toe."

"So much has happened since then that I feel it *was* a lifetime ago. I'm a different person than I was then. And you've made the difference."

He grinned. "Aw, shucks, ma'am."

"I'm serious, Sawyer. Thank you for all you've done for me. I truly appreciate it, but now I wonder—"

"You know, this is a pretty nice old tub since you fixed it up. I never asked, but what are you planning to do with it?"

She laughed. "I entertained some fantasy of poling it into the lake and drifting along like Huck Finn on his raft. I'm really—"

"Did I tell you that I have a boat? It's a

honey. I've had it in dry dock for repairs, but it'll be ready next week. You ever been scuba diving?"

She shook her head and opened her mouth to steer the subject back to her concerns, but he plunged on.

"Thought not. I'll teach you. You'll love it. I thought maybe for our hon—, I mean, pretty soon we could sail to the Florida Keys and spend a few days, then on down to the Caribbean. We could just loll in the sun and do some diving. How does that sound?"

"I don't know, it depends on—"

"Have you ever learned to skip rocks on water? I'll bet you haven't. Here, let me show you how." He sailed one of the pebbles toward the lake, and it skipped twice before submerging. "That wasn't my best effort, but you get the idea. Here, you try it. The secret is in the wrist action."

Taking the rock he offered, she made a halfhearted toss. Hers immediately plunked straight down.

"Why do I get the feeling that your heart isn't in this?" he asked.

"Because it isn't. I want to talk. I have some questions for you."

He tossed his handful of rocks off the

edge of the pier and took a deep breath. "I was afraid of that. I was hoping that you wouldn't ask. That you wouldn't *have* to ask." He crossed the gangplank to the houseboat and helped her onto the deck. His hands lingered on her waist.

"Ask what?"

"If I'd pursued you, spent time with you, made love to you just to get you to go to work for Mirth." He looked totally miserable. "I didn't. Swear to God. I'll swear on a stack of Bibles a mile high that I didn't."

"Why would I think that?"

"Because of what Herb said in the meeting this morning. I saw the way you glared at me."

She smiled up at him and cupped his cheek. "I know you didn't court me simply for Mirth. I'll admit that the thought flitted through my mind, but I dismissed it immediately. You're not that sort of person."

He looked as if the governor had granted him a last-minute reprieve. He broke into a huge grin. "Whew. You had me sweating bullets. If you didn't trust me, I didn't know how in the hell I was going to convince you." Engulfing her in a hug, he said, "Oh, sweetheart, I love you so much."

Lifting her onto the railing, he stepped between her legs. His lips were hungry as they moved over hers. His tongue plundered her mouth, and his hands moved restlessly over her back.

Her brain fogged. Rational thought fled ahead of the sensual onslaught of their kiss. Trailing his lips over her face and throat, he slipped a hand between their bodies to massage her breasts.

She moaned. He groaned.

He reached for the snap of her shorts.

"*Sawyer!* Not here. We're out in the open."

"Oh, hell. I look at you, and I want you," he murmured. "I touch you, and I go crazy. I hope there's a bunk inside the houseboat."

"There is."

"Good. Lock your legs around my waist."

"Yoo-hoo!" came a shout as he was about to lift her. "Yoo-hoo! Company!"

"That's Nan calling," Pip said.

"Oh, hell. I don't suppose that if we don't answer, she'll just give up and go away."

Pip giggled. "Not likely."

"I was afraid of that." He set her down and stepped away. "You go on to the house. I'll be there in a few minutes."

"Why can't you come with me now?"

He shot her a lopsided grin. "I need to do some adjusting and rearranging. If Nan got a look at my jeans now, she'd run me off with a broom."

Laughing, she scampered across the gangplank and jogged up the pier to where Nan waited with her arms folded across her ample middle.

Nan eyed her over the top of her glasses. "From where I stand, looks to me like I came along at the right time. Your uncles are here."

"Uncle Waldo and Uncle Emory?"

"Being them's the only uncles you got, yep. What's Sawyer doin' dawdlin' around down there?"

"He's . . . ah . . . checking the houseboat for leaks. He'll be along in a minute."

"Get on up to the house pretty quick. I got to go and stretch supper to feed two more."

Pip kissed the woman's cheek. "Thanks, Nan. I'll be right there."

They *did* look like aging versions of Tweedledum and Tweedledee, Sawyer thought as Pip introduced him to her uncles. Both sported tight-lipped smiles and had a slightly vacant look in their blue eyes, as if part of their attention was perennially preoccupied. Off in the worlds of math and physics, Sawyer imagined.

Only a few inches taller than Pip, they were identically rounded and identically dressed in dark slacks, white, short-sleeved dress shirts, and bow ties, except that Dr. Waldo LeBaron's tie was red and Dr. Emory LeBaron's was blue.

Sawyer shook hands with both men. "I'm happy to meet you. I've heard a lot about you from Pip. Bet it gets confusing with all those Doctor LeBarons around."

Waldo's belly shook with a strange little laugh that sounded almost like a Santa's. "No, we've worked it out. I'm Dr. Waldo . . ."

"And I'm Dr. Emory. Then there's Dr. John . . ."

"And you're Dr. Pip." Sawyer winked at her.

"Not exactly the proper address, some might say," Emory interjected, "but it makes things less confusing for the students at the university. Ho ho ho."

"You didn't perchance go to Rice, did you, Mr. Hayes?" asked Waldo. "Don't recall seeing you in any of my classes."

"My uncles think Rice is the only university of merit in the nation," Pip explained.

"Not so, not so. Harvard isn't half bad."

"No, sir, I didn't even attend Harvard. I didn't go to school at all."

"Didn't go to college? I say. And John tells me that you're president of your own company. Now isn't that something, Waldo?"

"It's something indeed."

Pip grinned. "Sawyer didn't go to school *at all*. Not even kindergarten."

"I say!"

"Sounds like an interesting story."

"It is," she said. "Sawyer, why don't you tell them about it while I see if Nan needs help with dinner?"

By the time everyone was seated around the table and eating, Sawyer had charmed the uncles the way he charmed everyone he met. Waldo and Emory had decided to make a long evening of it and announced that they were staying the night.

Uncle Waldo ho-hoed so vigorously at Sawyer's dramatic reenactment of the board meeting that his peas jiggled off his fork. "Wish I could have been there, don't you, Emory?"

"Yes, indeed. Off with his head!" he shouted, twirling his arm in the air. "You're a formidable opponent, Sawyer. How about a game of chess after dinner? Can use that new chess set Pip gave us."

Pip leaned over. "I should warn you that Uncle Emory is the faculty chess champion."

Sawyer winked at her. "I'm no slouch myself."

"Ho ho ho, Emory," Waldo said, "you may have met your match."

Emory rose, his napkin still tucked in the collar of his shirt, and started for the living room.

"Dr. Emory!" Nan said. "Sit yourself back down. That chess game can wait. Supper's not over yet, and we have lemon pie for dessert."

"Checkmate."

"I say, Waldo, he trounced me properly. Twice."

"Ho ho ho. About time, Sawyer. Rarely can beat him myself."

Sawyer stretched. "Lucky breaks."

"No, no. Nothing lucky about it. You're a fine player. Brilliant strategist. Isn't he, Waldo?"

"Brilliant."

"Well, I guess I'll call it a night," Sawyer said, nodding to the uncles. "Enjoyed meeting you." He shook hands with both of them and turned to Pip. "Walk me to the door?"

When they reached the porch, Pip said, "You made quite a hit with my uncles. Beating Uncle Emory at chess capped it. Why didn't you allow him to win?"

"Because he wouldn't have respected me."

She smiled. "You *are* a brilliant strategist."

"No grass growing under me."

"I know. All afternoon and evening you've skillfully evaded the conversation I wanted to have."

"I did? I thought we had it."

"Nope. Let's talk tomorrow."

He kissed her. "I'll see you in the morning. We can go see the boys and let them know that we've saved the ranch."

"I wasn't aware that they knew it was in jeopardy."

He chuckled. "They weren't. But we can go anyway. The boys are out of school tomorrow, and I promised I'd come. Mind?"

"Of course not. I always enjoy them."

"Would your uncles like to go along?"

Pip shook her head. "They'll be up and

gone by sunrise. They're very set in their routine. I was surprised by their visit. I suspect that they only came to check you out."

"Think I passed?"

"With an A-plus."

After a lingering good-night kiss, Pip stood at the door and watched him drive away. Questions and concerns still buzzed in her head, but she was too tired to focus on them tonight. Tomorrow.

At mid-morning the following day Sawyer landed the chopper in the clearing at the edge of the ranch. When the rotors stilled, he hopped out and came around to help Pip out.

She looked around. "I'm surprised that some of the boys aren't waiting for us. Scooter and Davy at least."

He shrugged. "Probably involved with something and didn't hear us landing. Come on." He grabbed her hand and took off at a fast clip.

"Slow down," she said, tugging on him to accommodate her short stride. "What's wrong with you? You've been acting strangely this morning."

"*Moi?* How?"

"I don't know exactly. Wired? Is that the term?"

"That's the term. Come on."

As they rounded the path, Pip saw all the boys, Matt, and the house parents gathered and waiting for them. When they drew closer, Matt raised a dented bugle to his lips and blew a *TA-ta-ta-TAAA-ta-TA*.

The boys stepped forward and, standing abreast, held up cards with words on them. In French the hand-lettered signs spelled out the message:

PIP, I LOVE YOU. PLEASE, WILL YOU MARRY ME? SAWYER

Tears sprang to her eyes. Shocked, she glanced from the message to Sawyer, who stood there, hands in his pockets, with a grin to rival the Cheshire Cat's.

"Well?" he asked.

"I—I don't know what to say. I'm dumbfounded."

Scooter and Davy ran forward with the SAWYER sign they held jointly. Beaming, Scooter said, "Did we do good, Sawyer? Did we do good?"

Sawyer ruffled Scooter's hair. "You did good. Perfect, in fact."

Scooter's snaggle-toothed grin widened. "Hear that, Davy? We was perfect." He turned to Pip. "Are you gonna marry us?"

Pip laughed. "*All* of you?" She glanced to the group that Matt was dispersing toward the house with shoos of his hands.

"Well, I guess mostly you're gonna marry Sawyer." He glanced over his shoulder to where Matt stood motioning with his hand. "We gotta go. Mister Matt said after we done our part, we should skedaddle and let you have some pri—pri—"

"Privacy?"

"Yeah, privacy." Scooter crooked his finger, and Pip leaned down. His arms snaked around her neck, and he planted a loud smack on one cheek. Davy stepped forward and shyly kissed the other. "We love you, Dr. Pip."

Around a huge lump in her throat, she said, "I love you too."

After one last hug the boys ran for the ranch house.

Sawyer kissed her cheek. "Don't I rate the same?"

"The same?"

"An 'I love you.' "

Silence.

"Do you love me?" he asked softly.

"Of course I do. I mean, I think I do. Yes, I must. But— Oh, I don't know what I mean. Sawyer, I'm so confused." Feeling generally flustered, she snuggled into his arms, seeking solace from the source of her distress.

He held her tightly and patted her back. "Confused about loving me or confused about marrying me?"

"I'm confused about everything. My life has turned upside down, and I don't have things sorted out. You can't imagine how unnerving this is for me."

He chuckled. "Poor darling."

She stiffened and tried to pull away. "My dilemma isn't amusing, Sawyer Hayes."

"Of course it isn't. Here, let's sit down and talk about this." He led her to a fallen log, and the two of them sat down. Gathering her close, with her head tucked under his chin, he said, "Tell me about it."

"Before you came along, my life was very orderly. I knew exactly who I was and where I was going. Oh, there was the hiatus to accommodate my social-development program, but that's all it was—a hiatus. My work has always been the focus of my life, and I intended for that to continue to be the case. I've been granted certain . . . gifts, and I have a responsibility to use those gifts in a productive way to contribute to society. But—"

"But—?"

"But now I've discovered another side to my personality. A side that likes—no, *needs*—to be completely carefree and irresponsible. You taught me how to play and have fun, and I've discovered that I like it. But I can't simply play forever, can I? I have my *work*, and— Oh, hell, I've never been so inarticulate in my entire life. My brain is a muddle. I don't know *who* or *what* I am anymore."

He stroked her and kissed the top of her head. "I know exactly who you are. You're the woman I love, the woman I want to marry and share the rest of my life with."

"But don't you understand? *I* don't know who that woman is. I don't know what I want to do the rest of my life. Everything used to be so clear, and now it's so cloudy. I don't know if I can accommodate your lifestyle into— Oh, Sawyer, I can't believe in luck or magic. And I've *never* seen a fairy." She burst into loud tears and burrowed her head closer to him, clutching fistfuls of his shirt.

"Shhh, sweetheart. Everything will be okay. We'll work it out. Don't cry." He tried to dry her tears with his shirttail. They kept coming and he kept mopping, all the while looking distressed. "What can I do to help? How can I make it better? Tell me."

"I don't know." She sniffed. "Time. I need some time to work things out. Time alone."

"Away from me, you mean?"

She nodded. "I think that would be best. When you're around, I get even more confused."

His smile didn't reach his eyes. Pain dulled their usual shining green. "How much time?"

"I don't know."

"Pip, I love you so damned much that I'll do anything to make you happy. If you want me to change, tell me how, and I'll do it. Whatever it takes, I'll do it."

"I couldn't ask that of you. You're wonderful the way you are and comfortable with who you are. You'd be miserable trying to change into something you're not. Just as I would. Just as anyone would. The problem isn't you. It's me . . . I think."

"Sounds like a bad case of identity crisis."

"Perhaps. But I have to deal with it before I can make any major decisions. I feel torn into pieces, and none of them fit together. There's a war going on inside me, and I'm losing. It's scary."

"Honey, I don't know what to tell you except that I love you. When did all this come about? Is it something I did, something I said? Something somebody else said or did? Lord, was it my mother?"

She shook her head. "It's been bothering me a bit for a while, but in the past couple of days it's gotten worse. Maybe I should go back to work. Immerse myself in the familiar. Do you think that would help?"

"The job is open for you at Mirth if you want it."

"Let me have some time to consider it. Time. There's that word again. Maybe that's all I need."

Sawyer sighed, not an impatient sigh but a resigned sigh. It made the lump in her throat swell. "You want to go visit with the boys today?" he asked quietly.

"I hate to disappoint them, but I don't think I can face them now. Do you think they'll understand?"

"Sure. No problem. I'll run tell them that you were so overcome by their performance that you swooned."

His remark coaxed a chuckle from her. *"Swooned?"*

"Yeah." He smiled faintly. "It was kind of a dumb idea, wasn't it? The cards, I mean. I had planned a much more romantic proposal in Acapulco with mariachis serenading and fireworks lighting the sky."

Overcome with tenderness, she touched his cheek and kissed him. "It was *not* dumb. It was very sweet." New tears stung her eyes and slowly trickled down her face. "I'm sorry."

Awkwardly he blotted her cheeks with his shirttail again. "Hey, don't sweat it. Everything's gonna be okay. I promise." He yanked his polo shirt off over his head and handed it to her. "You dry your eyes, and I'll be back in a flash."

"Sawyer! You can't go without your shirt."

"Sure I can." He trotted off toward the compound.

A powerful ache constricting her chest, she sat on the log and watched him go. Did she love him? Of course she loved him. Who wouldn't love Sawyer? He was the most lovable person she'd ever met. But he was a misfit. He seemed to live in a sort of Never-land that was out of step with the rest of the world she knew. But then, she'd always been a misfit too. The question was: Where did she belong?

She buried her face in his shirt, and the lingering smell of him permeated her senses. The thought of not being able to laugh and play and love with Sawyer was so overwhelming that she almost panicked. She almost ran after him to throw herself in his arms and never let go.

But she didn't.

Time.

She needed time to think, to reason things out without letting her emotions govern her decisions.

As Sawyer trotted toward the ranch buildings, he tried to come up with some excuse to give the boys. They would be as disappointed as he was. Disappointed, hell. He was beyond disappointed. He felt as if a giant had yanked his heart out and stomped on it.

It wasn't Pip's fault. It simply hadn't occurred to him that she wouldn't fall right in with his plans. And he'd had such plans. There was so much he wanted to do with her and for her. So many places he wanted to show her. So many things he wanted to share with her.

He'd been so sure that Pip was tailor-made for him, a gift from heaven to fill the lonely hole in his life. A budding kindred spirit. He was an arrogant ass! Had he screwed up everything?

Why did it have to be all *his* way? For the first time in a long while he questioned his own lifestyle, his own philosophy about the world. Was he irresponsible? Others had said often enough that he was.

But they didn't understand. They didn't have his inner vision.

He'd thought Pip could understand. But could she?

He could only hope . . . and pray . . . and wait.

ELEVEN

As he had for most of the past three days, Sawyer sat on his deck, stared out at the knoll where wildflowers bobbed in the wind, and absently stroked Shadow. With no effort, he could visualize Pip sitting there on a blanket, her face lifted to the sun, her hair fluttering in the breeze.

Her laughter echoed through the trees; her scent invaded his nostrils; her image filled his mind. If he closed his eyes, he could feel her touch, taste her sweetness. But they were only a poor illusion. He ached to see her in person. Without Pip, the magic had dimmed and was dying.

He'd promised her time. He'd sworn that

he wouldn't call her or contact her until she was ready. But he hadn't known that it would be this long or that the waiting would be this hard.

At the sound of his beeper, he started.

Was it she?

Quickly he checked the number. When his eyes lit on it, he let out such a whoop that Shadow shot out of his lap and zipped to safety under a table.

Snatching up the phone, he stabbed in Pip's number. As it rang, he took a deep breath and prayed like crazy.

When her sweet voice answered, his heart went to his throat, but he tried to sound calm. "Hi, honey. It's me. You ra-ng?"

"Uh, hello, Sawyer." Lord, her voice sounded wonderful. "About the consultant's job at Mirth—"

His heart dropped to his toes. "You decide to take it?"

"Well, no. I thought I should let you know that I decided that I'm not the best person for the job. But I talked to Bill Hruska, a colleague of mine, and he's interested. He's a big sports fan, and he played baseball in college. He's done some excellent work in the virtual reality field, and I think he would be perfect for the position."

For a moment he couldn't speak. He'd hoped . . .

"Sawyer, are you there?"

"I'm here. If you recommend this guy, I'm sure he'll be the best. Have him call Herb at his convenience." He waited for her to say more, but she didn't. "I've missed you," he said quietly.

"I've missed you too." Was that a catch in her voice? He damned sure had one in his.

"Got your thinking done?"

"Not yet."

"In the meantime how about a movie tonight? Or dinner? Or, hey, would you like to go sky-diving? I'll bet you'd be a natural. Or—"

"*Sawyer!*"

"You don't want to go to a movie with me?"

"It's best that I don't. I still need more time to think."

She was teetering in his direction. He knew it. She didn't have to call him about this Bill Woozits. She could have called Herb. But he didn't dare question her motive for phoning him. Patience, he told himself. Patience.

But patience was a pain in the butt. He was hurting. And what was worse, he knew that she damned well was too. It was times like this when all her intelligence got in the way.

"Well, I guess I'd better go," she said.

"Before you do, may I say one thing?"

"Of course."

"*Je t'aime*. Remember *that* while you're thinking. I love you, Pip, with everything that's in me. And while you're doing your soul-searching, look into your heart. See if you can find what I see there."

After a strangled noise, she hung up.

For the longest time Sawyer held the phone to his ear, listening to the dial tone. Oh, hell, had he blown it?

For the longest time, Pip sat with her hand on the phone, sniffing. Then she blew her nose and went back to her task.

Focusing on this short project for NASA sounded like just the thing to get her back into her work mode. John had said it was an intricate job and right up her alley. Ordinarily it would have been. She would have lost herself in the challenge. But now she didn't find it interesting at all. She had to force herself to work on it.

Oh, she could handle the project easily enough, but it was . . . boring.

A dozen times she'd found herself staring out the window, thinking about Sawyer, wondering where he was, what he was doing.

She'd called him on impulse, knowing that she could have easily passed Bill Hruska's name to Herb Burkhalter. But she didn't. She'd called Sawyer. Just to hear his voice.

Oh, hell, she thought. She was miserable. Why must life be so complicated? She had thought and thought about the situation and gotten nowhere. Maybe she needed an objective opinion.

Carol Venhuizen. She would call Carol.

With great effort she reined in her wandering thoughts and focused her complete attention on finishing the project.

Carol Venhuizen set down her coffee cup and smiled. "Sounds like an identity crisis to me. Textbook example of role confusion."

Pip chewed on her thumbnail. "That's what Sawyer said."

"Your Sawyer sounds like a bright man.

And it also sounds as if your crush has developed into considerably more."

Pip sighed. "I'm afraid so. Despite your warning, I lost my head."

Carol laughed. "Love does strange things to us. And you are in love with him, aren't you?"

"Totally, completely, madly. That's the only thing I'm sure about. But I wonder if love is always enough. Are our lifestyles compatible? That's a major issue."

"Only you can answer that."

"I was afraid that's what you were going to say. I've done a great deal of reading in the past few days, and I was wondering, do you think Sawyer suffers from the Peter Pan syndrome? Or is he simply allowing his inner child to express itself?"

"You *have* been doing lots of reading." Carol smiled. "Faddish ways to describe our personality and our behavior come and go. And many of them are contradictory. Let me ask you a few clarifying questions. Is Sawyer a selfish, narcissistic person?"

"Heavens, no. He's extremely generous and thoughtful. I've told you about the ranch, and also he donates time and money to a host of causes. Why, he dresses as a clown and visits Texas Children's Hospital at least once a month."

"I see. Is he rigid and demanding in his ideas or behavior?"

"*Sawyer*? He's the most flexible, undemanding person I know."

"Is he dependent or does he cling to other people?"

Pip shook her head.

"Is he successful in his business or occupation?"

"Very. He built Mirth from practically nothing. The games that still contribute the bulk of the company's profits are his creations. Of course his management style and work habits are terribly unconventional."

"Sounds typical of creative geniuses."

"It does?"

"Yes," Carol said. "Very typical. He must work sometime if he's invented all the things you say."

Pip drew her brows together. "I suppose he must. We've really never discussed it. All we ever did was play. He's very spontaneous, very lively. Being with him is always fun. He never takes life seriously. Except very serious things of course. He was livid about his uncle's takeover attempt."

"And he loves you and wants to marry you?"

"Yes."

Carol leaned forward and grinned. "Does he have a brother?"

"No, he was an only child."

Carol hooted with laughter.

"Why is that humorous?"

Clearing her throat, Carol said, "Never mind. Now I have a few questions about you. What moment in your life has brought you the greatest pleasure?"

Pip felt her cheeks redden.

"Besides that, what have you gotten the biggest kick out of?"

She thought for a moment. "Hang gliding in Acapulco."

"Second most?"

"Oh, maybe learning to ride a horse. Or roller-skating down Main Street at midnight."

"Even more exciting than when you received your Ph.D.? Than the important work you do?"

"Well, no, I suppose— Yes. Truthfully, yes. Much more exciting than the work I do."

"Why did you choose your field, or rather, fields?"

After pondering for a moment she said, "I really don't know. Perhaps because it was logical with my uncles being who they are. I had a quick mind, and I sort of fell into their mold. But I always enjoyed what I did—do," she amended quickly.

"Do you enjoy your work now?"

Pip sighed. "You know, I've been involved with a very challenging job for NASA, and"— she leaned closer—"it's boring as hell."

"How about your work projects in the past? Which did you enjoy most?"

"Devising computer games for kids. That was fun."

"Do you need the money from your work?"

"Not really. My pay has always been rather lucrative, but my expenses aren't much, and John has invested wisely for me. I suppose I could retire tomorrow if I chose. Money has never been of particular concern to me."

"Hmmm," Carol said. "Hmmm."

"What does that mean? Hmmm?"

"Psychologists' talk. It means either 'I haven't the foggiest notion' or 'It's all very clear to me, but you have to figure it out for yourself.' "

"That's no help."

Carol grinned. "Sure it is. Think about it. Think about what hang gliding and riding horses and . . . the other have in common. Forgetting about other people and their needs and expectations, think about what *you* want, what *you* like. Think about how you would prefer to spend the rest of your life if you knew it would end next month, or next year.

"Think about that, and I'll get the check."

That night and the next day Pip thought about everything that Carol had said. She thought about it constantly. She even dreamed about it. Dreamed of galloping on a spirited horse, her hair loose and streaming behind her as she laughed and raced the wind. Dreamed of soaring on a glider like an eagle, high over mountaintops. Dreamed of skating on a golden highway that went on and on and on.

When she awakened, the thrill of her experiences lingered. The heady sense of exhilaration made her feel marvelous, powerful. Free.

Until she remembered that she had to go to NASA and finish the project. She suddenly felt bound and heavy. Constricted.

That bothered her. Badly.

Before she thought, she picked up the phone and dialed, then hung up.

In less than a minute the phone jingled, and Sawyer said, "You ra-ng?"

"I have a question for you. A serious question."

"Shoot."

"Do you ever work?"

He laughed. "Of course I work. I work like a son-of-a-gun when the mood strikes me. But to me most of the work I do is fun. I enjoy it."

"You *do*?"

"Sure. But I like to play too. In fact I prefer to play most of the time. Want me to come over and play with you?"

"*Sawyer!* Be serious. Don't you ever feel *guilty* about not working more like other people?"

"Lord, no. Why should I feel guilty? Honey, I learned a long time ago that I heard a different drummer."

"Oh. Well, thanks. Good-bye."

A few seconds after she hung up, the phone rang again.

"Want to tell me what all that was about?" Sawyer asked.

"I'm simply trying to get some things straight in my mind. You were very helpful."

"Wanna go to the beach today? We could drive down to Galveston and build sand castles."

She sighed. "I have to work."

It was well after midnight when Pip drove up in front of the lake house. She'd gotten lost on the maze of freeways downtown and driven around for hours until she'd found the correct route. She'd been preoccupied as always. But about matters far different from those that usually absorbed her.

She trudged inside, kicked off her shoes, and climbed the stairs. One thing that she'd discovered—a shocking thing—was that her job-satisfaction rating was zero. It had never occurred to her that she didn't like her work, that it wasn't fulfilling.

Stupid, she knew, but there it was. She didn't belong where she'd been. Constricted.

She had a hunch that Sawyer knew all along.

Sawyer.

How she longed to see him, talk to him, touch him. He filled her thoughts as she prepared for bed. Once under the covers, she reached for the phone, then drew her hand back. She couldn't call at this hour.

Then she grinned. He wouldn't care.

She dialed his beeper number, then waited.

And waited.

And waited.

He must be asleep.

Disappointed, she propped herself up in bed and picked up a book about developmental stages. Six four-leaf clovers fluttered out from between the pages. She'd pressed the ones she had found. Carefully she replaced each delicate plant, smiling as she remembered the day. They *had* brought her luck. They'd brought her a whole new beginning.

She turned off the lamp, snuggled under the covers, and dreamed of fairies.

At least she thought it was a dream. A tiny creature in gauzy garb and with lacy wings flitted around the room, glowing like a firefly. "Come on," the fairy said in a little bell-like voice. She beckoned with an impatient motion of her arm. "Come on. Let's fly. Let's fly."

Pip jerked awake with her arms outspread, smiling and ready to follow.

When she realized where she was, her head dropped back down to the pillow. She turned over and was about to drift off again when she heard a noise against her window.

A *ping*. Then another. And another.

Her heart began to race furiously. Leaping from her bed, she ran to the window and raised it.

There sat Sawyer astride the oak limb and grinning. "You ra-ng?"

She laughed. "I did."

"Have you finished your thinking?"

"I looked into my heart."

"And?"

She flung out her arms. "I want to *fly*!"

He laughed. "Come fly with me, love. Come fly with me beyond the stars."

Giddy with excitement, she threw on some clothes, scribbled a note for Nan, and climbed down the tree with Sawyer.

The note, which was propped against her pillow, said:

I'VE GONE TO NEVER-LAND WITH SAWYER. DON'T EXPECT ME BACK.

TWELVE

In the wee hours of the morning Sawyer landed the chopper at the yacht basin and helped Pip down from her seat. Hugging her, he swung her around, laughing and feeling high as a kite.

"Tell me again," he said. "In English."

"I love you. With all my heart and soul, I love you."

"And?"

"And, yes, I'll marry you."

He threw back his head and crowed.

"*Sawyer!* People will think we're nuts."

He grinned. "Do we care?"

She laughed. "Not a bit."

"Come on. I want to show you something." Tugging her along, he headed for a large sailboat moored at the basin. On the pier he flourished his arm toward the vessel. "This is how we're traveling to the Caribbean. Like it?"

She squinted into darkness held at bay by only dim lighting. "I can't see it very well, but I'm sure it's lovely."

"And it has a lovely cabin with a lovely bed." He grinned. "Wanna see?"

"Sure. I'm game."

But Pip didn't get a good look at the cabin until much, much later. As soon as they were inside, he took her into his arms and kissed her with a hunger that curled her toes. She returned his kiss just as hungrily, savoring the chocolaty taste of him, the woodsy smell of him, the hard feel of him, and greedy for more.

"Oh, love," he murmured, "I've missed you so much. Don't ever keep me away again. I couldn't stand it."

"I won't. I missed you just as much."

"I was afraid you'd never get your thinking done. I was planning to kidnap you if you waited much longer."

"Kidnap me?"

"Yep." He kissed her again, running his hands over her body as if he couldn't get enough of touching her.

"You knew, didn't you? You always knew."

"That we were kindred spirits? That we were soul mates? Yes, I knew. I've loved you forever."

With fumbling fingers, they stripped away clothes and scruples and all the old baggage. They made love as if it were the first time.

They flew beyond the stars.

And at dawn they hoisted the sails and headed for their own Never-land, the sun gleaming on the name of the boat—*It's Magic.*

THE EDITOR'S
CORNER

Celebrate the most romantic month of the year with LOVESWEPT! In the six fabulous novels coming your way, you'll thrill to the sexiest heroes and cheer for the most spirited heroines as they discover the power of passion. It's all guaranteed to get you in the mood for love.

Starting the lineup is the ever-popular Fayrene Preston with **STORM SONG**, LOVESWEPT #666— and Noah McKane certainly comes across like a force of nature. He's the hottest act in town, but he never gives interviews, never lets anyone get close to him—until Cate Gallin persuades the powerfully sensual singer to let her capture him on film. Nobody knows the secret they share, the bonds of pain and emotion that go soul-deep . . . or the risks they're taking when Cate accepts the challenge to reveal his stunning talent—without hurting the only man she's ever loved. This compelling novel is proof positive of why Fayrene is one of the best-loved authors of the genre.

SLIGHTLY SHADY by Jan Hudson, LOVE-SWEPT #667, is Maggie Marino's first impression of the brooding desperado she sees in the run-down bar. On the run from powerful forces, she's gotten stranded deep in the heart of Texas, and the last thing she wants is to tangle with a mesmerizing outlaw who calls himself Shade. But Shade knows just how to comfort a woman, and Maggie soon finds herself surrendering to his sizzling looks—even as she wonders what secret he's hiding. To tantalize you even further, we'll tell you that Shade is truly Paul Berringer, a tiger of the business world and brother of the Berringer twins who captivated you in **BIG AND BRIGHT** and **CALL ME SIN**. So don't miss out on Paul's own story. Bad boys don't come any better, and as usual Jan Hudson's writing shines with humor and sizzles with sensuality.

Please give a warm welcome to Gayle Kasper and her very first LOVESWEPT, **TENDER, LOVING CURE**, #668. As you may have guessed, this utterly delightful romance features a doctor, and there isn't a finer one than Joel Benedict. He'd do anything to become even better—except attend a sex talk seminar. He changes his mind, though, when he catches a glimpse of the teacher. Maggie Springer is a temptress who makes Joel think of private lessons, and when a taste of her kissable lips sparks the fire beneath his cool facade, he starts to believe that it's possible for him to love once more. We're happy to be Gayle's publisher, and this terrific novel will show you why.

Sally Goldenbaum returns to LOVESWEPT with **MOONLIGHT ON MONTEREY BAY**, #669. The beach in that part of California has always been special to Sam Eastland, and when he goes to his empty house there, he doesn't expect to discover a beautiful nymph. Interior decorator Maddie Ames fights to convince him that only she can create a sanctuary to soothe his troubled spirit . . . and he's too spellbound to refuse. But when their attraction flares into burning passion and Sam fears he can't give Maddie the joy she deserves, she must persuade him not to underestimate the power of love. Vibrant with heartfelt emotion, this romance showcases Sally's evocative writing. Welcome back, Sally!

A spooky manor house, things that go bump in the night—all this and more await you in **MIDNIGHT LADY**, LOVESWEPT #670, by Linda Wisdom. The granddaughter of the king of horror movies, Samantha Lyons knows all about scare tactics, and she uses them to try to keep Kyle Fletcher from getting the inside scoop about her family's film studio. But the devastatingly handsome reporter isn't about to abandon the story—or break the sensual magic that has woven itself around him and beautiful Sam . . . even if wooing her means facing down ghosts! Hold on to your seats because Linda is about to take you on a roller-coaster ride of dangerous desires and exquisite sensations.

It **LOOKS LIKE LOVE** when Drew Webster first sees Jill Stuart in Susan Connell's new LOVESWEPT, #671. Jill is a delicious early-morning surprise, clad in silky lingerie, kneeling in Drew's uncle's yard, and coaxing a puppy into her arms. Drew knows instantly that she wouldn't have to beg him to come running, and he sets off on a passionate courtship. To Jill, temptation has never looked or felt so good, but when Drew insists that there's a thief in the retirement community she manages, she tells him it can't be true, that she has everything under control. Drew wants to trust her, but can he believe the angel who's stolen his heart?

Susan delivers a wonderful love story that will warm your heart.

Happy reading!

With warmest wishes,

Nita Taublib

Nita Taublib
Associate Publisher

P.S. Don't miss the exciting women's novels from Bantam that are coming your way in February—**THE BELOVED SCOUNDREL** by nationally bestselling author Iris Johansen, a tempestuous tale of abduction, seduction, and surrender that sweeps from the shimmering halls of Regency England to the decadent haunts of a notorious rogue; **VIXEN** by award-winning author Jane Feather, a spectacular historical romance in which an iron-willed nobleman suddenly becomes the guardian of a mischievous, orphaned beauty; and **ONE FINE DAY** by supertalented Theresa Weir, which tells the searing story of a second chance for happiness for Molly and Austin Bennet, two memorable characters from Theresa's previous novel **FOREVER**. We'll be giving you a sneak peek at these terrific books in next month's LOVESWEPTs. And immediately following this page look for a preview of the exciting romances from Bantam that are *available now!*

Don't miss these exciting books by your
favorite Bantam authors

On sale in December:

DESIRE
by *Amanda Quick*

LONG TIME COMING
by *Sandra Brown*

STRANGER IN MY ARMS
by *R.J. Kaiser*

WHERE DOLPHINS GO
by *Peggy Webb*

And in hardcover from Doubleday
AMAZON LILY
by *Theresa Weir*

Amanda Quick

New York Times bestselling author of
DANGEROUS and **DECEPTION**

DESIRE

This spectacular novel is Amanda Quick's first medieval romance!

*From the windswept, craggy coast of a remote British isle comes
the thrilling tale of a daring lady and a dangerous knight who are
bound by the tempests of fate and by the dawning of desire . . .*

"There was something you wished to discuss with me, sir?"

"Aye. Our marriage."

Clare flinched, but she did not fall off the bench. Under
the circumstances, she considered that a great accomplishment. "You are very direct about matters, sir."

He looked mildly surprised. "I see no point in being
otherwise."

"Nor do I. Very well, sir, let me be blunt. In spite of
your efforts to establish yourself in everyone's eyes as the
sole suitor for my hand, I must tell you again that your
expectations are unrealistic."

"Nay, madam," Gareth said very quietly. "'Tis your
expectations that are unrealistic. I read the letter you sent
to Lord Thurston. It is obvious you hope to marry a phantom, a man who does not exist. I fear you must settle for
something less than perfection."

She lifted her chin. "You think that no man can be found who suits my requirements?"

"I believe that we are both old enough and wise enough to know that marriage is a practical matter. It has nothing to do with the passions that the troubadours make so much of in their foolish ballads."

Clare clasped her hands together very tightly. "Kindly do not condescend to lecture me on the subject of marriage, sir. I am only too well aware that in my case it is a matter of duty, not desire. But in truth, when I composed my recipe for a husband, I did not believe that I was asking for so very much."

"Mayhap you will discover enough good points in me to satisfy you, madam."

Clare blinked. "Do you actually believe that?"

"I would ask you to examine closely what I have to offer. I think that I can meet a goodly portion of your requirements."

She surveyed him from head to toe. "You most definitely do not meet my requirements in the matter of size."

"Concerning my size, as I said earlier, there is little I can do about it, but I assure you I do not generally rely upon it to obtain my ends."

Clare gave a ladylike snort of disbelief.

"'Tis true. I prefer to use my wits rather than muscle whenever possible."

"Sir, I shall be frank. I want a man of peace for this isle. Desire has never known violence. I intend to keep things that way. I do not want a husband who thrives on the sport of war."

He looked down at her with an expression of surprise. "I have no love of violence or war."

Clare raised her brows. "Are you going to tell me that you have no interest in either? You, who carry a sword with a terrible name? You, who wear a reputation as a destroyer of murderers and thieves?"

"I did not say I had no interest in such matters. I have, after all, used a warrior's skills to make my way in the world. They are the tools of my trade, that's all."

"A fine point, sir."

"But a valid one. I have grown weary of violence, madam. I seek a quiet, peaceful life."

Clare did not bother to hide her skepticism. "An interesting statement, given your choice of career."

"I did not have much choice in the matter of my career," Gareth said. "Did you?"

"Nay, but that is—"

"Let us go on to your second requirement. You wrote that you desire a man of cheerful countenance and even temperament."

She stared at him, astonished. "You consider yourself a man of cheerful countenance?"

"Nay, I admit that I have been told my countenance is somewhat less than cheerful. But I am most definitely a man of even temperament."

"I do not believe that for a moment, sir."

"I promise you, it is the truth. You may inquire of anyone who knows me. Ask Sir Ulrich. He has been my companion for years. He will tell you that I am the most even-tempered of men. I am not given to fits of rage or foul temper."

Or to mirth and laughter, either, Clare thought as she met his smoky crystal eyes. "Very well, I shall grant that you may be even-tempered in a certain sense, although that was not quite what I had in mind."

"You see? We are making progress here." Gareth reached up to grasp a limb of the apple tree. "Now, then, to continue. Regarding your last requirement, I remind you yet again that I can read."

Clare cast about frantically for a fresh tactic. "Enough, sir. I grant that you meet a small number of my requirements if one interprets them very broadly. But what about our own? Surely there are some specific things you seek in a wife."

"My requirements?" Gareth looked taken back by the question. "My requirements in a wife are simple, madam. I believe that you will satisfy them."

"Because I hold lands and the recipes of a plump perfume business? Think twice before you decide that is sufficient to satisfy you sir. We live a simple life here on Desire. Quite boring in most respects. You are a man who is no doubt accustomed to the grand entertainments provided in the households of great lords."

"I can do without such entertainments, my lady. They hold no appeal for me."

"You have obviously lived an adventurous, exciting life," Clare persisted. "Will you find contentment in the business of growing flowers and making perfumes?"

"Aye, madam, I will," Gareth said with soft satisfaction.

"'Tis hardly a career suited to a knight of your reputation, sir."

"Rest assured that here on Desire I expect to find the things that are most important to me."

Clare lost patience with his reasonableness. "And just what are those things, sir?"

"Lands, a hall of my own, and a woman who can give me a family." Gareth reached down and pulled her to her feet as effortlessly as though she were fashioned of thistledown. "You can provide me with all of those things, lady. That makes you very valuable to me. Do not imagine that I will not protect you well. And do not think that I will let you slip out of my grasp."

"But—"

Gareth brought his mouth down on hers, silencing her protest.

LONG TIME COMING
by
SANDRA BROWN

Blockbuster author Sandra Brown—whose name is almost synonymous with the *New York Times* bestseller list—offers up a classic romantic novel that aches with emotion and sizzles with passion . . .

For sixteen years Marnie Hibbs had raised her sister's son as her own, hoping that her love would make up for the father David would never know . . . dreaming that someday David's father would find his way back into her life. And then one afternoon Marnie looked up and Law Kincaid was there, as strong and heartbreakingly handsome as ever. Flooded with bittersweet memories, Marnie yearned to lose herself in his arms, yet a desperate fear held her back, for this glorious man who had given her David now had the power to take him away. . . .

The Porsche crept along the street like a sleek black panther. Hugging the curb, its engine purred so deep and low it sounded like a predator's growl.

Marnie Hibbs was kneeling in the fertile soil of her flower bed, digging among the impatiens under the ligustrum bushes and cursing the little bugs that made three meals a day of them, when the sound of the car's motor attracted her attention. She glanced at it over her shoulder, then panicked as it came to a stop in front of her house.

"Lord, is it that late?" she muttered. Dropping her trowel, she stood up and brushed the clinging damp earth off her bare knees.

She reached up to push her dark bangs off her forehead before she realized that she still had on her heavy gardening gloves. Quickly she peeled them off and dropped them beside the trowel, all the while watching the driver get out of the sports car and start up her front walk.

Glancing at her wristwatch, she saw that she hadn't lost track of time. He was just very early for their appointment, and as a result, she wasn't going to make a very good first impression. Being hot, sweaty, and dirty was no way to meet a client. And she needed this commission badly.

Forcing a smile, she moved down the sidewalk to greet him, nervously trying to remember if she had left the house and studio reasonably neat when she decided to do an hour's worth of yard work. She had planned to tidy up before he arrived.

She might look like the devil, but she didn't want to appear intimidated. Self-confident friendliness was the only way to combat the disadvantage of having been caught looking her worst.

He was still several yards away from her when she greeted him. "Hello," she said with a bright smile. "Obviously we got our signals switched. I thought you weren't coming until later."

"I decided this diabolical game of yours had gone on long enough."

Marnie's sneakers skidded on the old concrete walk as she came to an abrupt halt. She tilted her head in stunned surprise. "I'm sorry, I—"

"Who the hell are you, lady?"

"Miss Hibbs. Who do you think?"

"Never heard of you. Just what the devil are you up to?"

"Up to?" She glanced around helplessly, as though the giant sycamores in her front yard might provide an answer to this bizarre interrogation.

"Why've you been sending me those letters?"

"Letters?"

He was clearly furious, and her lack of comprehension only seemed to make him angrier. He bore down on her like a hawk on a field mouse, until she had to bow her back to look up at him. The summer sun was behind him, casting him in silhouette.

He was blond, tall, trim, and dressed in casual slacks and a sport shirt—all stylish, impeccably so. He was wearing opaque aviator glasses, so she couldn't see his eyes, but if they were as belligerent as his expression and stance, she was better off not seeing them.

"I don't know what you're talking about."

"The letters, lady, the letters." He strained the words through a set of strong white teeth.

"*What* letters?"

"Don't play dumb."

"Are you sure you've got the right house?"

He took another step forward. "I've got the right house," he said in a voice that was little more than a snarl.

"Obviously you don't." She didn't like being put on the defensive, especially by someone she'd never met over something of which she was totally ignorant. "You're either crazy or drunk, but in any case, you're *wrong*. I'm not the person you're looking for and I demand that you leave my property. Now."

"You were expecting me. I could tell by the way you spoke to me."

"I thought you were the man from the advertising agency."

"Well, I'm not."

"Thank God." She would hate having to do business with someone this irrational and ill-tempered.

"You know damn well who I am," he said, peeling off the sunglasses.

Marnie sucked in a quick, sharp breath and fell back a step because she did indeed know who he was. She raised a hand to her chest in an attempt at keeping her jumping heart in place. "Law," she gasped.

"That's right. Law Kincaid. Just like you wrote it on the envelopes."

She was shocked to see him after all these years, standing only inches in front of her. This time he wasn't merely a familiar image in the newspaper or on her television screen. He was flesh and blood. The years had been kind to that flesh, improving his looks, not eroding them.

She wanted to stand and stare, but he was staring at her with unmitigated contempt and no recognition at all. "Let's go inside, Mr. Kincaid," she suggested softly.

STRANGER IN MY ARMS
by
R.J. KAISER

With the chilling tension of Hitchcock and the passionate heat of Sandra Brown, STRANGER IN MY ARMS is a riveting novel of romantic suspense in which a woman with amnesia suspects she is a target for murder.

Here is a look at this powerful novel . . .

"Tell me who you are, Carter, where you came from, about your past—everything."

He complied, giving me a modest summary of his life. He'd started his career in New York and formed a partnership with a British firm in London. When his partners suffered financial difficulties, he convinced my father to buy them out. Altogether he'd been in Europe for twelve years.

Carter was forty, ten years older than I. He'd been born and raised in Virginia, where his parents still resided. He'd attended Dartmouth and the Harvard Business School. In addition to the villa he had a house in Kensington, a flat off the avenue Bosquet in Paris, and a small farm outside Charlottesville, Virginia.

After completing his discourse, he leaned back and sipped his coffee. I watched him while Yvonne cleared the table.

Carter Bass was an attractive man with sophistication and class. He was well-spoken, educated. But mainly he appealed to me because I felt a connection with him, tortured though it was. We'd been dancing around each other since he'd appeared on the scene, our history at war with our more immediate and intangible feelings toward each other.

I could only assume that the allure he held for me had to do with the fact that he was both a stranger and my husband. My body, in effect, remembered Carter as my mind could not.

I picked up my coffee cup, but paused with it at my lips. Something had been troubling me for some time and I decided to blurt it out. "Do you have a mistress, Carter?"

He blinked. "What kind of a question is that?"

"A serious one. You know all about me, it's only fair I know about you."

"I don't have a mistress."

"Are you lonely?"

He smiled indulgently. "Hillary, we have an unspoken agreement. You don't ask and neither do I."

"Then you don't want to talk about it? I should mind my own business, is that what you mean?"

He contemplated me. "Maybe we should step out onto the terrace for some air—sort of clear our mental palate."

"If you like."

Carter came round and helped me up. "Could I interest you in a brandy?"

"I don't think so. I enjoyed the wine. That's really all I'd like."

He took my arm and we went through the salon and onto the terrace. He kept his hand on my elbow, though I was no longer shaky. His attention was flattering, and I decided I liked the changing chemistry between us, even though I had so many doubts.

It was a clear night and there were countless stars. I inhaled the pleasantly cool air and looked at my husband. Carter let his hand drop away.

"I miss this place," he said.

"Did I drive you away?"

"No, I've stayed away by choice."

"It's all so sad," I said, staring off down the dark valley. "I think we're a tragic pair. People shouldn't be as unhappy as we seem to be."

"You're talking about the past. Amnesiacs aren't supposed to do that, my dear."

I smiled at his teasing.

"I'm learning all about myself, about us, very quickly."

"I wonder if you're better off not knowing," he said, a trace of sadness in his voice.

"I can't run away from who I am," I replied.

"No, I suppose you can't."

"You'd like for me to change, though, wouldn't you?"

"What difference does it make? Your condition is temporary. It's probably better in the long run to treat you as the person I know you to be."

His words seemed cruel—or at least unkind—though what he was saying was not only obvious, it was also reasonable. Why should he assume the burden of my sins? I sighed and looked away.

"I'd like to believe in you, Hillary," he said. "But it isn't as simple as just giving you the benefit of the doubt."

"If I could erase the past, I would." My eyes shimmered. "But even if you were willing, *they* wouldn't let me."

Carter knew whom I was referring to. "They" were the police, and "they" were coming for me in the morning, though their purpose was still somewhat vague. "They" were the whole issue, it seemed to me—maybe the final arbiter of who I really was. My past not only defined me, it was my destiny.

"I don't think you should jump to any conclusions," he said. "Let's wait and see what they have to say."

He reached out and took my bare arms, seemingly to savor the feel of my skin. His hands were quite warm, and he gripped me firmly as he searched my eyes. I was sure then that he had brought me to the terrace to touch me, to connect with me physically. He had wanted to be close to me. And maybe I'd come along because I wanted to be close to him.

There were signs of desire in Carter's eyes. Heat. My heart picked up its beat when he lowered his mouth toward mine. His kiss was tender and it aroused me. I'd hungered for this—for the affirmation, for the affection—more than I knew. But still I wasn't prepared for it. I didn't expect to want him as much as I did.

I kissed Carter every bit as deeply as he kissed me. Then, at exactly the same moment, we pulled apart, retreating as swiftly as we'd come together. When I looked into his eyes I saw the reflection of my own feelings—the same doubt, distrust, and fear that I myself felt.

And when he released me, I realized that the issues separating us remained unresolved. The past, like the future, was undeniable. The morning would come. It would come much too soon.

WHERE DOLPHINS GO
by
PEGGY WEBB

"Ms. Webb has an inventive mind brimming
with originality that makes all of her books
special reading."
—*Romantic Times*

*To Susan Riley, the dolphins at the Oceanfront Research Center
were her last chance to reach her frail, broken child. Yet when she
brought Jeffy to the Center, she never expected to have to contend
with a prickly doctor who made it clear that he didn't intend to
get involved. Quiet, handsome, and hostile, Paul Taylor was a
wounded man, and when Susan learned of the tragedy behind his
anguish, she knew she had to help. But what began as compassion
soon turned to desire, and now Susan was falling for a man who
belonged to someone else....*

"A woman came to see me today," Bill said. "A woman and
a little boy."

Paul went very still.

"Her name is Susan . . . Susan Riley. She knew about the
center from that article in the newspaper last week."

There had been many articles written about Dr. Bill
McKenzie and the research he did with dolphins. The most
recent one, though, had delved into the personality of the
dolphins themselves. An enterprising reporter had done his
homework. "Dolphins," he had written, "relate well to people. Some even seem to have extrasensory perception. They
seem to sense when a person is sick or hurt or depressed."

"Her little boy has a condition called truncus arteriosus . . ." Bill squinted in the way he always did when he
was judging a person's reaction.

Paul was careful not to show one. *Truncus arteriosus. A condition of the heart. Malfunctioning arteries. Surgery required.*

"Bill, I don't practice medicine anymore."

"I'm not asking you to practice medicine. I'm asking you to listen."

"I'm listening."

"The boy was scheduled for surgery, but he had a stroke before it could be performed."

For God's sake, Paul. Do something. DO SOMETHING!

"Bill . . ."

"The child is depressed, doesn't respond to anything, anybody. She thought the dolphins might be the answer. She wanted to bring him here on a regular basis."

"You told her no, of course."

"I'm a marine biologist, not a psychologist." Bill slumped in his chair. "I told her no."

"The child needs therapy, not dolphins."

"That's what I thought, but now . . ." Bill gave Paul that squinty-eyed look. "You're a doctor, Paul. Maybe if I let her bring the boy here during feeding times—"

"No. Dammit, Bill. Look at me. I can't even help myself, let alone a dying child and a desperate mother."

Bill looked down at his shoes and counted to ten under his breath. When he looked up Paul could see the pity in his eyes.

He hated that most of all. . . .

Susan hadn't meant to cry.

She knew before she came to the Oceanfront Research Center that her chances of success were slim. And yet she had to try. She couldn't live with herself if she didn't do everything in her power to help Jeffy.

Her face was already wet with tears as she lifted her child from his stroller and placed him in the car. He was so lifeless, almost as if he had already died and had forgotten to take his body with him. When she bent over him to fasten the seat belt, her tears dripped onto his still face.

He didn't even notice.

She swiped at her tears, mad at herself. Crying wasn't going to help Jeffy. Crying wasn't going to help either of them.

Resolutely she folded the stroller and put it in the backseat. Then she blew her nose and climbed into the driver's seat. Couldn't let Jeffy know she was sad. Did he see? Did he know?

The doctors had assured her that he did. That the stroke damage had been confined to areas of the brain that affected his motor control. That his bright little mind and his personality were untouched. And yet, he sat beside her like some discarded rag doll, staring at nothing.

Fighting hard against the helpless feeling she sometimes got when she looked at Jeffy, she turned the key in the ignition and waited for the old engine to warm up. She was not helpless. And she refused to let herself become that way.

"Remember that little song you love so much, Jeffy? The one Mommy wrote?" Jeffy stared at his small sneakers.

Sweat plastered Susan's hair to the sides of her face and made the back of her sundress stick to the seat.

"Mommy's going to sing it to you, darling, while we drive." She put the car into gear and backed out of the parking space, giving herself time to get the quiver out of her voice. She was *not* going to cry again. "You remember the words, don't you, sweetheart? Help Mommy sing, Jeffy."

" 'Sing with a voice of gladness; sing with a voice of joy.'" Susan's voice was neither glad nor joyful, but at least it no longer quivered. Control was easier in the daytime. It was at night, lying in the dark all by herself, when she lost it. She had cried herself to sleep many nights, muffling the sounds in the pillow in case Jeffy, sleeping in the next room, could hear.

" 'Shout for the times of goodness.' " How many good times could Jeffy remember? " 'Shout for the time of cheer.' " How many happy times had he had? Born with a heart condition, he had missed the ordinary joys other children took for granted—chasing a dog, kicking a ball, tumbling in the leaves, outrunning the wind.

" 'Sing with a voice that's hopeful . . .' " Susan sang on, determined to be brave, determined to bring her child back from that dark, silent world he had entered.

As the car took a curve, Jeffy's head lolled to the side so he was staring straight at her. All the brightness of childhood that should be in his eyes was dulled over by four years of pain and defeat.

Why do you let me hurt?

The message in those eyes made her heart break.

The song died on her lips, the last clear notes lingering in the car like a party guest who didn't know it was time to go home. Susan turned her head to look out the window.

Biloxi was parching under the late afternoon sun. Dust devils shimmered in the streets. Palm trees, sagging and dusty, looked as tired as she felt. It seemed years since she had had a peaceful night's sleep. An eternity since she had had a day of fun and relaxation.

She was selfish to the core. Thinking about her own needs, her own desires. She had to think about Jeffy. There must be something that would spark his interest besides the dolphins.

And don't miss these heart-stopping
romances from Bantam Books,
on sale in January

THE BELOVED SCOUNDREL
by the nationally bestselling author
Iris Johansen
"You'll be riveted from beginning to end
as [Iris Johansen] holds you captive to a
love story of grand proportions."
—*Romantic Times* on
The Magnificent Rogue

VIXEN
by **Jane Feather**
A passionate tale of an iron-willed
nobleman who suddenly becomes the
guardian of a mischievous, orphaned
beauty.

ONE FINE DAY
by **Theresa Weir**
"Theresa Weir's writing is poignant,
passionate and powerful. *One Fine Day*
delivers intense emotion and compelling
characters that will capture the
hearts of readers."
—*New York Times* bestselling
author Jayne Ann Krentz

OFFICIAL RULES

To enter the sweepstakes below carefully follow all instructions found elsewhere in this offer.

The **Winners Classic** will award prizes with the following approximate maximum values: 1 Grand Prize: $26,500 (or $25,000 cash alternate); 1 First Prize: $3,000; 5 Second Prizes: $400 each; 35 Third Prizes: $100 each; 1,000 Fourth Prizes: $7.50 each. Total maximum retail value of Winners Classic Sweepstakes is $42,500. Some presentations of this sweepstakes may contain individual entry numbers corresponding to one or more of the aforementioned prize levels. To determine the Winners, individual entry numbers will first be compared with the winning numbers preselected by computer. For winning numbers not returned, prizes will be awarded in random drawings from among all eligible entries received. Prize choices may be offered at various levels. If a winner chooses an automobile prize, all license and registration fees, taxes, destination charges and, other expenses not offered herein are the responsibility of the winner. If a winner chooses a trip, travel must be complete within one year from the time the prize is awarded. Minors must be accompanied by an adult. Travel companion(s) must also sign release of liability. Trips are subject to space and departure availability. Certain black-out dates may apply.

The following applies to the sweepstakes named above:

No purchase necessary. You can also enter the sweepstakes by sending your name and address to: P.O. Box 508, Gibbstown, N.J. 08027. Mail each entry separately. Sweepstakes begins 6/1/93. Entries must be received by 12/30/94. Not responsible for lost, late, damaged, misdirected, illegible or postage due mail. Mechanically reproduced entries are not eligible. All entries become property of the sponsor and will not be returned.

Prize Selection/Validations: Selection of winners will be conducted no later than 5:00 PM on January 28, 1995, by an independent judging organization whose decisions are final. Random drawings will be held at 1211 Avenue of the Americas, New York, N.Y. 10036. Entrants need not be present to win. Odds of winning are determined by total number of entries received. Circulation of this sweepstakes is estimated not to exceed 200 million. All prizes are guaranteed to be awarded and delivered to winners. Winners will be notified by mail and may be required to complete an affidavit of eligibility and release of liability which must be returned within 14 days of date on notification or alternate winners will be selected in a random drawing. Any prize notification letter or any prize returned to a participating sponsor, Bantam Doubleday Dell Publishing Group, Inc., its participating divisions or subsidiaries, or the independent judging organization as undeliverable will be awarded to an alternate winner. Prizes are not transferable. No substitution for prizes except as offered or as may be necessary due to unavailability, in which case a prize of equal or greater value will be awarded. Prizes will be awarded approximately 90 days after the drawing. All taxes are the sole responsibility of the winners. Entry constitutes permission (except where prohibited by law) to use winners' names, hometowns, and likenesses for publicity purposes without further or other compensation. Prizes won by minors will be awarded in the name of parent or legal guardian.

Participation: Sweepstakes open to residents of the United States and Canada, except for the province of Quebec. Sweepstakes sponsored by Bantam Doubleday Dell Publishing Group, Inc., (BDD), 1540 Broadway, New York, NY 10036. Versions of this sweepstakes with different graphics and prize choices will be offered in conjunction with various solicitations or promotions by different subsidiaries and divisions of BDD. Where applicable, winners will have their choice of any prize offered at level won. Employees of BDD, its divisions, subsidiaries, advertising agencies, independent judging organization, and their immediate family members are not eligible.

Canadian residents, in order to win, must first correctly answer a time limited arithmetical skill testing question. Void in Puerto Rico, Quebec and wherever prohibited or restricted by law. Subject to all federal, state, local and provincial laws and regulations. For a list of major prize winners (available after 1/29/95): send a self-addressed, stamped envelope entirely separate from your entry to: Sweepstakes Winners, P.O. Box 517, Gibbstown, NJ 08027. Requests must be received by 12/30/94. DO NOT SEND ANY OTHER CORRESPONDENCE TO THIS P.O. BOX.